WOLF GOD

Of Wolves and Fae: Book One

Lily Tate

TTB THOMAS TELLER BOOKS

TTB | THOMAS TELLER BOOKS

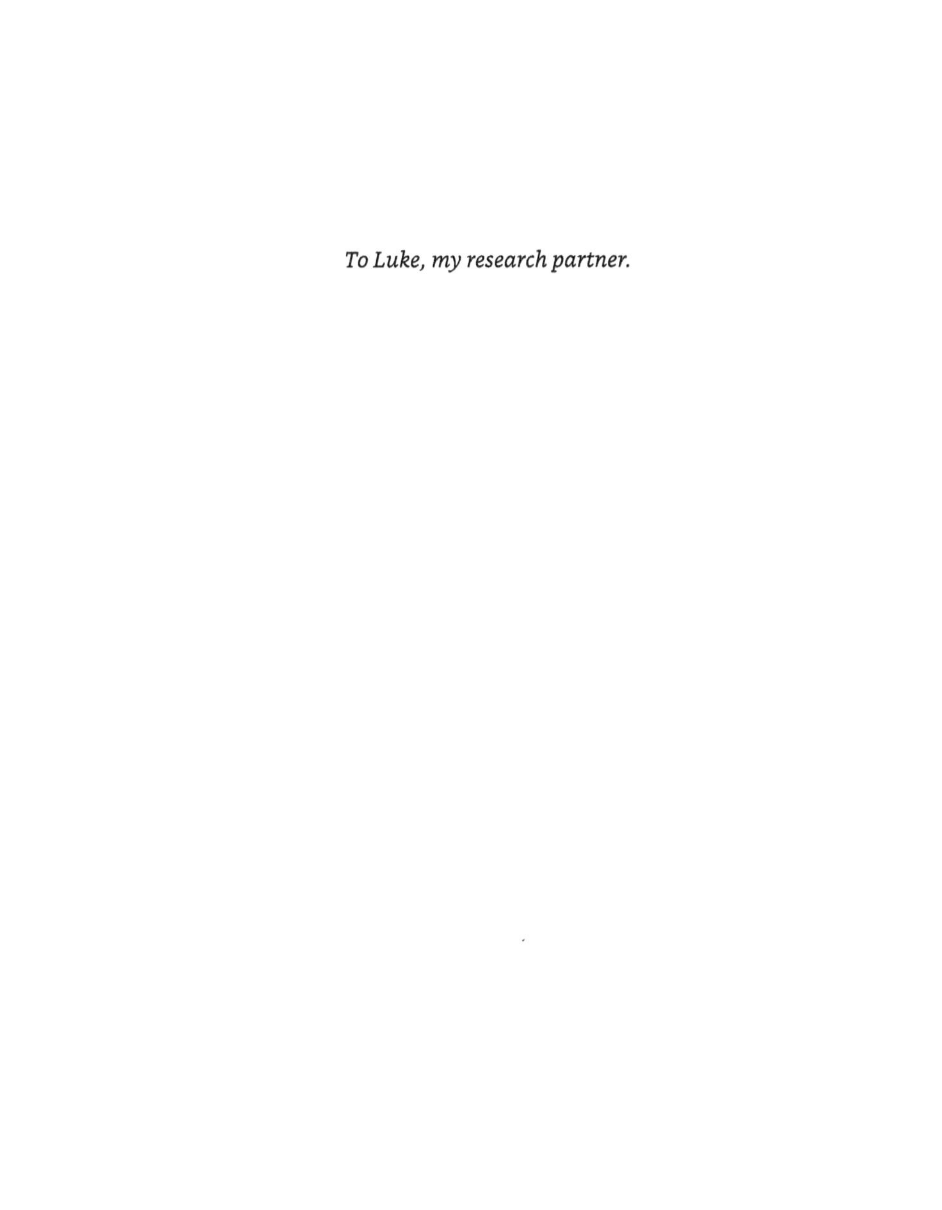

To Luke, my research partner.

CONTENTS

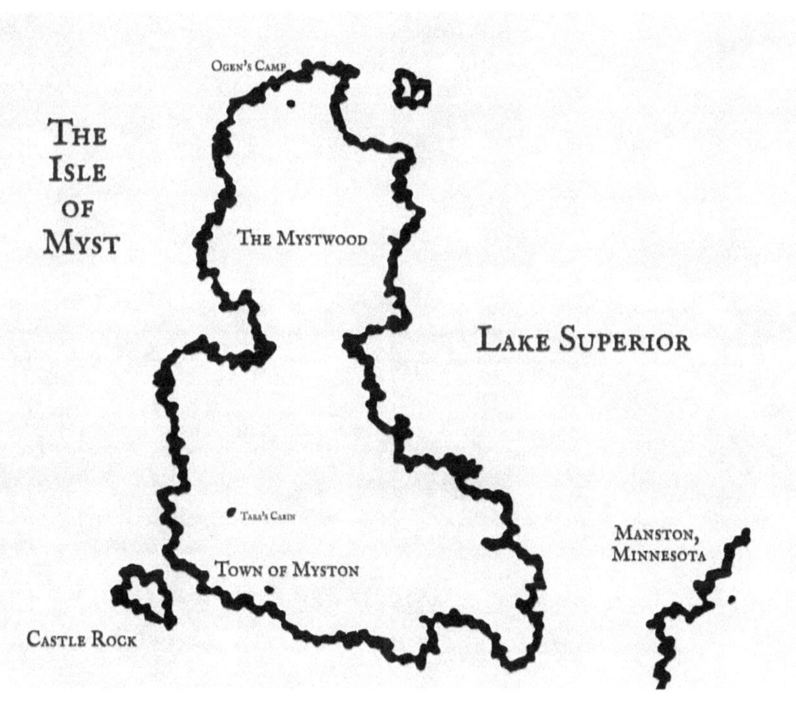

THE
ISLE
OF
MYST
OGEN'S CAMP
THE MYSTWOOD
LAKE SUPERIOR
TARA'S CABIN
TOWN OF MYSTON
MANSTON,
MINNESOTA
CASTLE ROCK

PROLOGUE

The creature stood over me, naked: his skin was pale as winter, his eyes as black as coals. Black wings sprouted from his back, melding with the shadows around him. "Anastasia," he whispered.

I was laying on my back before him, in a field of winter snow. I was naked, and my light brown skin was stark against the ice. I stared at him, at his plump lips and perfectly sculpted face; he was like a prince from a fairy tale, only darker... dangerous magic roiled off of him in waves. It slid over me, exciting every cell in my body. His body was slim but strong, with rounded muscles and hard cut lines. He looked like a roman statue, carved from marble. His cock was hard and massive, pressing up into the air, searching for me.

I spread my legs for him, revealing the warmth there.

He smiled, his perfect teeth as sharp as blades. His black wings flapped once, twice, then settled behind his back and vanished. He crept towards me, then crouched, crawling the rest of the way. I watched as his mouth kissed the inside of my leg, felt the hot blood there. His kisses moved inward until his lips grazed my the lips between my legs. I felt his tongue inside me, cold as winter, and I shivered.

The pleasure moved through me in waves, electricity washing over my nerves. I squirmed, but he clamped his mouth down on my opening, moving his tongue faster.

He stopped just as the heat was building in my belly, begging me to come.

I opened my eyes and looked down at him. His dark eyes

stared up from between my legs, his lips glistening with my wetness. He spoke, and his voice was like the roar of a winter storm.

"You will be my queen, Anastasia," he said.

He crawled upward until his perfect, god-like face hovered above mine. I felt his rock hard cock against me, the tip of it teasing between my folds.

"Please…" I whispered.

"You will be my bride," he said, "and you will bear my sons."

I felt the tip slide slowly in, and I gasped. It felt so cold, but the power coming off of him was like a dark sun, burning bright.

He sunk himself to the hilt, and I moaned in pleasure.

"Farien…" I whispered.

"My love," he said as he thrust into me, "my mate."

"Yes!" I screamed. His thrusts grew more rapid. His pale, strong hands wrapped around my wrists, bearing down on me. His face twisted into a mask of rage as he thrust into me one more time, then shuddered. His black wings erupted from his back, and I came too, shivering as the pleasure took over my body.

He stroked my cheek, and I stared into his night-dark eyes.

"Come to me, my love," he whispered.

Then the shadows swallowed him, and the dream vanished.

CHAPTER 1

I fled. It was dark, in a forest I couldn't recognize; blood pounded in my chest and I heaved for air. The night was cold and pitch black, save for the full moon piercing the canopy of pines. It illuminated a forest floor of gray-green needles, moss covered boulders, twisting roots like serpents.

I didn't know what was going on; in one moment, I was hitchhiking to Chicago. The next, I was having a very strange — and sexy— dream. And then, I woke up in a decrepit house in this forest, next to a sleeping pack of wolves. And not ordinary wolves; wolves the size of horses. *Shifters.*

A wolf's howl pierced the night air. Following me.

I ran faster, breath heaven in my chest, burning as it entered. My legs pumped like pistons. I might have been small, but I was quick and lean from years on the streets. But I was no match for the monsters chasing me.

Behind me, the wolves pounded through the night. *I can't keep up with them,* I thought, *I can't outrun a pack of shifters.* But neither could I fight.

My clothes were tattered and dirty; my left sneaker was torn, ripping off as I ran, threatening to trip me. And more than that?

I was soaked in blood.

It was sticky on my hands and face, drenching my clothes. But none of it seemed to be mine.

What happened to me in there? I thought.

Suddenly, gunshots pierced the air. The bullets sprayed the boulder next to me, turning granite into dust. I dove behind it, breathing deeply, gasping for any air. Behind me, human voices and guttural growls came closer. I poked my head behind the stone, only to see hulking shapes running through the forest towards me. Their heads were wolf-like, but their bodies were human, their bodies muscle clad and covered in hair. *Hybrid form,* I thought. *Shit. They must be powerful.*

Time for some tricks of my own.

I concentrated, drawing on the well of magic inside me. It appeared as a blue light, and orb that floated in my mind's eye, like a miniature sun. I drew on that well, drawing magic into my hands. Then I closed my eyes, extended my hands, and reached outwards for the water in the air, in the soil.

Rise, I commanded.

The water responded to me like a well trained dog. Miniature droplets lifted from the soil, like a reverse rain. They hovered there. Most witches and some element that came naturally to them. Water had always been my element.

Conceal me, I commanded, pushing my magic into the thought, crafting reality to my will.

The drops of water exploded into mist.

Suddenly, the forest vanished, replaced by a thick fog.

I heard shouts and angry yells behind me. "Where'd she go?" Someone screamed.

I smirked and ran through the mist, disappearing into the wood. *Mist won't stop them from smelling you,* I thought.

Bullets sprayed again, this time more randomly. They ricocheted off stones, embedded into the ancient trees; their thunder made my eardrums rattle, and a low whine replaced the sounds of the world.

The mist followed me, as I commanded it, concealing me in its darkest parts. I sprinted, breath heaving, not sure how much longer I could run.

Then, a shape: a black military jacket. A man, not

seemingly a shifter, staring at me. He looked surprised, lost in the mist. When he saw me, he opened his mouth to scream and raised his rifle to shoot.

I closed my eyes. I didn't want to kill him — and he'd have to *not* be a shifter for it to work, anyway. Shifters had magic in them — that's what allowed them to shift — so casting spells directly on their bodies wouldn't work. Humans, however...

I reached out, called to the magic inside me. Again, it responded, that bright blue light.

Blood is mostly water, I thought.

And I called out to the blood inside him and said, *Boil.*

A scream. Agonizing. The man's face went from pale white to burning red, and fissures opened on his skin where the blood steamed out. His eyes went bloodshot, then totally black, and he collapsed the the ground. Dead.

I'm sorry, I thought, *I'm so sorry.*

Shouts from behind me; they'd heard the man's dying screams.

"There!" They shouted.

I sprinted away, leaping over the man's still-smoking corpse.

The mist followed, and I focused, making it flare out from me, giving me a space of a few feet that I could see. *I need to get out of here. Away from them. But where is here? And who are they?*

Bullets sprayed again. Then, to my right, a flash of bright light.

Fire spread all around me, consuming the woods in a liquid flame. Glass shards and burning alcohol stuck to my thigh, burning through the bloody fabric. I screamed. *Molotov cocktails? Seriously? Are these mobster werewolves or what?*

"There!" A deep voice growled. Bullets sprayed again, and in the distance I saw more hybrid forms sprinting at the edges of my mist.

Then, a growl above all of them. "She's mine!" The voice shook me; it was deep and edged with power.

A huge shape appeared in the mist: a wolf form even larger

than the others. The shifter was the size of a minivan, with moon-white fur. Instantly, I could feel the power radiating off hom.

Recognition flared in me, followed by fear. *Him.*

I didn't remember who he was, not exactly, except that I should be *very* afraid of him.

I turned on heel and ran, the pain flaring in my leg. I grit my teeth and ran harder than ever before, even as my body begged for me to give up. My limbs felt leaden and heavy. My eyes flickered as unconsciousness threatened.

Don't stop. Whatever you do, Ana, don't stop.

Then, above the shouts and the growls and the spray of bullets: a tinkling. A rushing. The lap of waves.

Water.

My home. My element.

If I could only reach it.

* * *

There! I saw the stream and beyond it, the sea: an endless expanse of wine-dark water.

I pounded my legs faster, leapt over the stream —

And fell.

I crashed to the dirt, the stone shore knocking all the wind out of me.

I turned over, painfully, lifting myself up on one arm.

The mist around me dissipated as I lost my concentration. Then, before me, appearing in the vanishing mist, was the wolf.

He was huge, twice the size of some other shifters I'd seen. His fur was snow-white, matted with mud in places. And his body was covered in pink scars, criss-crossing here and there. One large claw mark covered his left eye, which was missing; only an empty socket covered with scar tissue remained. His other eye was emerald green, and power flickered there, glowing in the darkness. His maw opened, and I saw huge white teeth glittering. Saliva dripped from his canines as he snapped.

To my surprise, his animal mouth formed human words: "Leaving so soon?" he said.

And he lunged at me.

His powerful back legs reared, shot him forward, over the stream. His front paws extended, claws arcing like wicked blades. His jaws opened wide, showing blood red tongue and pearl white teeth. A growl slipped from his lips as he prepared to slash open my throat.

I called out to my magic. It responded in a panic, welling inside me with more power than I'd ever felt, the fear augmenting and sharpening my skill.

Protect me! I commanded.

I lifted a hand and splayed my fingers. Blue-white light glowed from my hand, and I heard a distant hum, like electricity.

The water in the stream flashed in an instant. It exploded upwards in spikes like a wolf's teeth.

Then it froze into wicked icicles, impaling the white wolf through its chest.

The wolf howled, stuck in midair, icicles piercing its torso. Blood dripped down them, making the clear ice a sickening red. The wolf twitched and growled, staring at me with hate in its golden eye. *That won't be enough to kill him,* I thought. *Maybe for an ordinary shifter. But something feels… powerful, about this one.*

Then, in the distance, more shouts. The others were coming.

I stood, limping towards the shore. The water called out to me like a siren.

Bullets. They splashed into the water, sending clouds of vapor into the night. They clattered against the stones, breaking them into shrapnel.

Then, a prick. Like a needle.

I looked down, only to see a red stain spreading from my chest. It bloomed like a flower around a single bullet hole.

This time, the blood was mine: new blood, mixing with whoever's blood stained my clothes.

Oh, I thought.

Then I collapsed into the water, and let the current carry me away.

CHAPTER 2

The water carried me; somehow, without me commanding it, my magic took me out to sea. Or what I thought was a sea. The water was fresh and cold, with no smell of salt. I slept, my magic allowing me to breathe even through the water. How, I wasn't sure; the night passed in a dream, slipping in and out of consciousness. The cold didn't bother me, either; my magic enveloped me in a warm light, keeping the icy waves at bay. The world rolled in and out in currents, replacing reality with dreams and dreams with reality. I dreamed of the one eyed white wolf, saying: Leaving so soon?

How long had I been there, in that camp? How had I gotten there in the first place?

The dreams shifted and suddenly I was on the shore, feeling rocks under my numb fingers. I coughed up water, sputtering on the sand. When I looked up, a shadow of a man was standing above me: broad and strong. He bent down, picked me up, and I smelled him: musk and leather and warm coffee. Then I collapsed into darkness again, cradled in his arms.

Hours — or maybe days — later, I awoke on a hard cot. I sat up, wincing at the pain in my stomach. The small room came into view: five gray walls, and one that was covered in bars.

A jail cell? I thought. I'd been in jail before, of course, but usually I remembered getting in trouble. Who puts a defenseless, injured, rescued girl in a jail cell? Even one covered in blood?

I looked down. I was wearing an oversized white t-shirt and a pair of pink jogging shorts. They were clean, mercifully, and smelled alright. I distantly wondered what had happened to my old clothes, and my dad's jacket. *Those fuckers better not have thrown it out. You can get blood out of leather. It just takes a little water magic.*

I pulled up the huge white t-shirt and looked at my stomach: bandages were wrapped firmly around the spot, and it wasn't as painful as I'd thought it would be. I lowered the t-shirt and looked at my thigh: similarly, the burn from the Molotov cocktail was wrapped in bandages and wet with some kind of salve. *Seriously,* I thought, *who uses Molotov cocktails? Am I in frickin' Russia?*

I examined the room. It was small and hardly used, with a clean green blanket on the cot and a toilet in the corner. Outside the bars, a lone desk sat, stacked with papers. No one sat there, and I couldn't see down the hall. I stood, moved to the bars, and stuck my nose through them, trying to get a better angle. Nothing.

I moved to the cot. Above it, set high in the wall, was a small window. This, too, was covered in iron bars. I stood on the cot, got onto my tip-toes, and looked out. All I could see was the tips of pine trees and a single sign for a dinky diner.

I'm in a town, at least, I thought, *not trapped in some rotting house in the woods. But why am I in jail? And how did I get here in the first place?*

I tried to think back. I'd been hitchhiking my way from Cleveland to Chicago. Not that bad of a trip; the work had dried up out East, so I was heading West. The grapevine told me that witch services were going for a premium in LA, so I decided to give it a shot. I'd been on the highway, holding my thumb up... then what?

I shook my head.

The memory ended there.

Memory magic? I wondered, *could someone have abducted*

me and taken my memories? They'd need a witch or warlock to do it. How did I even wake up, then? I should still be chained to that wall.

I slumped down on the cot. My stomach rumbled. When was the last time I ate? The magic I used during the fight with the white wolf had drained me. Not to mention whatever my magic had done while I was unconscious, to keep me alive underwater. When I reached for my magic, it was less like a miniature sun and more like a weak candle flame. I doubted that I'd be able to break out of the cell, even if I could get my hands on some water.

If they took my memories, they could've taken more.

I tried to recount all the details I could about myself.

Anastasia Walker. Twenty one years old. Water witch. Born in Pennsylvania, live on the road. Parents, dead. Brother, dead.

At least I remembered all the important parts.

I laid back on the cot and tried not to cry. That was a lesson I'd learned early on, living on the streets. Crying did no one any good. Instead, I rested. At some point, I must have fallen asleep, because I awoke to the sound of a gruff voice. A man's voice.

"Wake up, sweetheart," he said.

I opened my eyes and stared at the most beautiful man I had ever seen.

His face was chiseled and square, and blue eyes burned out from beneath thick eyebrows. He was tan, with a close cropped beard and luscious dark brown hair. He wore a policeman's uniform, dark blue. His chest was broad, and I could see where his muscles pressed against the fabric. Similarly, his powerful thighs seemed barely contained by the blue trousers. I tried not to look at the way he barely fit into the uniform. Did he dress like that *only* to be insanely sexy?

Other than that, he looked like any other small town cop. Just a million times hotter. He looked a little tired, a little fed up, with messy hair and a perpetually disappointed expression. The hot, 'disappointed dad' energy made me made want to collapse into a puddle. He wore a badge on his chest that read: Sheriff Pearson.

Still, my instincts took over: that's what years of living on the street will do to you. I shot up, gritting past the pain in my stomach, and raised a hand, ready to summon magic. I reached into myself, ready to use what little magic I had to defend myself. Instead, when I touched my magic, I felt a jolt of pain like an electric shock. I yelped and brought my hand back to my chest.

"What the *fuck?*" I said.

The sexy sheriff just laughed. I watched his stupid grin form stupid dimples around his stupid perfect smile. "You won't be able to pull off any magic in here, kid. The cell is warded."

I frowned, then summoned my second sight. The room glowed for a moment, everything becoming outlines of blue light. I saw circular wards of faerunes covering the floor, ceiling, and walls. Even the iron bars were carved with invisible runes. *That's tricky magic, imbuing iron,* I thought, *why does a small town sheriff have access to a skilled artificer?*

I turned to look at him, my second sight still activated. Within the outline of his blue form, I saw a shimmering second image: that of the wolf spirit that was bonded to him.

I jerked back, onto the cot, ready to fight. *Shifter,* I thought. *Did the one eyed wolf capture me after all?*

"Whoah, whoah. No need to panic. I won't hurt you," he said. I dropped my witch's sight and looked at the man before me. The wolf spirit bonded to him vanished. All I saw was the deceptively handsome man, grinning cockily.

"Wolf shifter," I said.

He raised his hands. "Got me," he said. Then he turned slightly, without taking his eyes off me, and said: "Grayson, can you come in here?"

From the hallway, a second man appeared. He wore green medical scrubs and carried a large first aid kit. This man, too, was handsome, albeit in a different way. He was tall and lean, with wiry muscle and pale skin. Long blonde hair hung shaggily over his eyes. I let my witch's sight take over for a second, and saw that he had a mountain lion spirit bonded to him. *Another shifter,* I thought.

"Grayson here is the town vet. He's the one that stitched you up. Would be a real shame if you kept moving and tearing out your stitches. Right?"

I stared at him, said nothing. Grayson took a step forward.

I leapt from the cot into a standing position. No way in hell I was letting these guys put their hands on me. I shivered at the thought of me, unconscious, with two strange men working under my clothes.

"Whoah — it's okay," Grayson said, "I'm just going to check the stitches. Then I'll leave. Okay?"

The hot cop sighed and leaned against the wall of the cell. "If we wanted you dead, why would we go through all the trouble of patching you up? We could have left you on that beach to freeze to death. Or bleed to death. Or just wait for whoever shot you to find you, I guess."

So they don't work for the one eyed wolf. Or they want me to think they don't.

"Then why lock me in a cell?" I spat, "If you're so noble, why am I behind bars that are warded against a magic."

"Because an unknown witch washed up on our island? And we have no idea who you are?" Hot Cop said.

I frowned. *Island.* Not exactly an easy place to run from.

I looked back and forth between them. Grayson seemed concerned. Hot Cop just seemed irritated. I didn't believe a word they said. When people locked you up, they usually didn't mean well towards you. And I hated being in a cage. Not to mention, I'd just been chased by wolf shifters. For all I knew, this could be some elaborate ruse by the very same people I'd just escaped from. Hot Cop didn't seem to know who shot me, but like I said, you learn not trust people, when you grow up alone.

"Two shifters, and you have a warded jail cell just for witches. Where am I?" I asked.

Grayson and Hot Cop looked to one another.

"That's classified," Hot Cop said.

"Classified? What are you, CIA? You uniform tells me you're more likely from the Federal Bureau of Ingesting Donuts."

"Oh, so you must be a comedian," Hot Cop said, "that's one thing we know about you, I guess. Tell me, what's Jerry Seinfeld like in real life?"

He leaned forward, mocking sincerity.

"No, here's how it's going to go, sweetheart — you're going to tell us who you are. Then we'll decide whether we keep you here or throw you back in the lake."

The lake. An island in a lake. Where, Lake Michigan? Lake Superior? That would mean I'm not that far from Chicago. Still, how did I even get here? And where was the one eyed wolf keeping me?

"Why don't we all just calm down," Grayson said. He seemed gentle. I had a witch's intuition, which tended to be pretty good at reading people. And Grayson's vibe seemed calm and simple. A healer, through and through. Hot Cop, on the other hand, screamed alpha. Everything he said was a thinly veiled command; he was used to getting exactly what he wanted. *And I'm sure plenty of women are willing to give it to him,* I thought.

Grayson turned to me, opening his first aid kit. "Look — I need to change the bandages on your leg. And apply salve. If you don't trust me, fine, but it still has to get done. So I'm going to roll the bandages and the salve over to you, and you can do it yourself."

Grayson fixed me with gentle eyes; eyes any woman would kill to see hovering over them in bed. Something told me he'd be a very gentle, generous lover. Hot Cop on the other hand…

"Jesus Christ…" Hot Cop grumbled.

I nodded. Grayson rolled over the bandages and the salve, and I started undoing the old wrap. The wound under was red and angry, sticky with salve. Some scab had formed at the corners. *How long have I been asleep?* I wondered.

"If you could show me the bullet wound, that would help too. I just need to know the stitches haven't come out," Grayson said. Again, he spoke low and slow. I nodded again, and finished applying the salve and bandages to my leg. Then I peeled off the oversized white t-shirt. I was still wearing my ratty sports bra underneath. It smelled awful, and was stained with sweat and blood. *At least they had the decency not to take my bra off,* I thought.

I put the shirt to the side, and watched Hot Cop turn away, cheeks flushed. Maybe they flickered back for just a moment, but I pretended not to notice.

Grayson just continued looking at me like I was a stray dog, wounded on the side of the road. I didn't like being looked at like a puppy. I peeled off the old bandages around my stomach, wincing as I did so. Beneath, a mess of stitches covered the area just above my belly button. The wound was red and raw, pinched together by black stitches.

"It looks okay — for now. But soon I'll have to change it. We can cross that bridge when we get to it," Grayson said. He stood. "Keep the salve and the bandages, in case you need to change them again."

I nodded.

Hot Cop scowled. "Not even a thank you? This guy spent hours with you, stitching you up. You're lucky the bullet didn't hit anything important."

"I didn't ask for your help," I spat.

"You couldn't, because you were unconscious," Hot Cop said, "would you rather have had us let you die?"

"If it saved me from another second listening to you preach at me? Yeah, maybe," I said.

Hot Cop rolled his eyes, pushed off the wall. "Come on, Grayson, let's go," he said, "maybe a few hours in a warded cell will make her willing to talk."

A few hours, I thought, *and I've already been out for maybe a full day. How long will it take that pack of wolf shifters to track me down?*

"Wait," I said, as they both turned around. I closed my eyes. I didn't want to give them my full name, but I didn't want to lie to them, either.

"I'm… Ana," I said, "I don't know how I washed up on your island. I was hitchhiking, and then there's a long stretch I don't remember, and I woke up in the woods. Some wolf shifters were hunting me. I escaped, but one of them did this." I gestured to my wounds.

"And?" Hot Cop asked.

"And that's all I remember," I said, "that's the truth."

Grayson and Hot Cop shared a significant look.

"Wolf shifters, you said?" Grayson asked. "How many?"

"I don't know. But you can see why I'm suspicious of this one," I nodded towards Hot Cop. He stood with his arms folded, biceps bulging in the tight uniform. A look of conservation clouded his face.

"Our guys?" Grayson asked Hot Cop quietly.

"No way. Hunting an innocent girl?"

"Duluth pack?" Grayson asked.

"I'll send out some feelers, but it doesn't sound like them, either," he said.

Duluth. Duluth, Minnesota. We must be close to there. No wonder that water was so fucking cold.

"Do you remember anything else? Anything at all?" Hot Cop asked, his voice urgent.

I opened my mouth, ready to tell them about the mercenaries with automatic rifles or the white, one eyed wolf. Instead, I kept it shut. I still didn't trust them, and I wasn't ready to show my hand.

"No," I said, "that's it."

Hot Cop looked at me appraisingly, scanning up and down.

"What do we do now?" Grayson asked.

"Keep her here. I need to talk to the mayor," he said, "figure out what to do."

"Keep me here? Are you fucking kidding? Those wolves could be at the door any minute!" I said. I stood, wincing again.

"I doubt that. We're pretty... out of the way, here. You'll be safe," Hot Cop said.

"You don't know that," I growled.

He shrugged. "Tough shit. I'll come get you when we've made a decision."

He stepped out the cell. Grayson followed, casting one forlorn look at me before he left. Then Hot Cop closed the sliding cell door behind him and locked it.

"And sweetheart? In the future, you should remember something my momma taught me. When you want something, you'll catch more flies with honey than with vinegar."

He smirked.

"What's that supposed to mean?" I asked, angrily.

"It means stop being so fucking difficult," he said. Then he walked away, leaving me in my cell.

CHAPTER 3

Hours passed in the cell. Hot Cop left me with some paperback mystery books, an extra blanket, and a space heater. He brought me lunch and a cup of shitty coffee, which I begrudgingly accepted. I wolfed down the sandwich, chips, and coffee in a few heartbeats. Afterwards, I lay down and read for what seemed like hours. I tried my magic again, but the wards simply shocked me. I used my second sight to examine the faerunes for weak spots, but my knowledge of runes was absolute shit. I was self taught, and my magic worked mostly on intuition and whatever I could find online. I had enough raw power to make up for my lack of training, but there was no way I was breaking out a cell built by a master artificer. Instead I paced, and plotted my escape.

If we really were on an island, that complicated things. Even if I did escape the cell, I'd have to make it to the coast. Then, I'd need to figure out how to replicate whatever magic had carried me safely to the island. When a witch is in serious danger, sometimes her magic will take over — but I tried to cross the lake consciously, using only my own skills, I might wind up drowning. That was if Hot Cop didn't catch me first, or the One Eyed Wolf didn't track me down.

I sighed, having paced myself to exhaustion. I felt like a caged animal, and I hated being caged. All my life had been about avoiding feeling trapped. Keeping on the road, moving from city to city, only staying long enough to work a few jobs and then move on. No friends, no family, and certainly no boyfriends. I'd learned that no one could be trusted with my safety but me. Having your parents slaughtered in front of you will do that.

Grayson and Hot Cop returned, unlocking the door. They stepped in, carrying another tray of food: this time a chicken Caesar salad and a coke. My stomach grumbled just looking at it.

Grayson looked to Hot Cop, who nodded at him. He turned to face me. "It's time to change your bandages. Are you ready?"

I nodded and sat up, removing my shirt again. This time, I removed my bra too.

"Whoah!" Hot Cop said, turning away.

"Sorry," I said, innocently, "I thought it would get in the way. And the bra is filthy."

Grayson looked at me and visibly gulped. He bit his lip, summoning his medical professional passivity, and knelt down to change my bandages.

I let my eyes flicker towards Hot Cop. He still looked away, giving the little lady her privacy. *A small town gentleman,* I thought. *Perfect.*

I gripped the severed cord of the space heater behind my back. It didn't seem like either of them had noticed it wasn't humming, pushing out heat into the cell. I didn't have any illusions that I could take Hot Cop or Grayson, for that matter. But I was quick, and I was clever.

"Sorry about this," I said quietly. Grayson looked up, confused.

I leapt onto his back, grabbed his wrists, and tied them behind his back with the shoddily made handcuffs. *Thank god for Girl Scouts,* I thought, tightening the knot.

"Hey, what the—" Grayson started. But it was too late. He was already bound and on his knees, with a shard of shattered coffee cup pressed to his jugular.

"Whoah, whoah!" Grayson said.

Hot Cop turned, eyes wide. He stared at me, pressing that ceramic shard into Grayson's throat. "First rule of keeping someone in jail, dumbass," I said, "never give them something that could be used as a weapon."

Hot Cop stared at me, then lifted his hand towards me. The other rested on his service weapon.

"Uh uh," I said, pressing the shard into Grayson's throat. He winced. A thin stream of blood dripped down his long white neck. "Slide it over."

Hot Cop looked from me to Grayson, then back again. Slowly, he took the pistol out of its holster, then placed it on the ground. He slid it over to me across the concrete floor. "There. Now let him go," Hot Cop growled.

I kept my eyes on Hot Cop as I crouched to the floor, still holding the shard to Grayson's neck. With my free hand, I reached for the pistol and picked it up. In a fluid motion, I dropped the shard and raised the gun, kicking Grayson onto the floor. He landed with a thud and a gasp.

"Okay, sweetheart," Hot Cop said, "what now?"

"Now, you stop calling me 'sweetheart.' Got it?" I said.

He frowned. "I—"

"Save it. Now take off your pants."

Hot Cop blinked. "What?" He asked.

"Take off your pants. Shirt, too."

"I don't really see why—"

"Hey. Who is holding the gun?" I wiggled it, just as a reminder. "You kept me in a freezing cold cell in my underwear. Now, I'm going to return the favor."

His eyes narrowed. Then, grudgingly, he stripped off his uniform. He unbuttoned his shirt first, then tore the white undershirt over his head. I had to stop myself from gasping as I saw his bare chest: tan, covered in course hair, with heavy pecs and firm abs. Not too cut, with just the right amount of beef. His hard belly arced in a graceful V-shape down beneath his pant line. My eyes followed the thick line of dark hair towards what lay beneath it.

"Pants,"I said.

He unbuttoned his slacks and then slipped them down. He

wore nothing but white underwear beneath, clean and fresh. *At least he's not a slob,* I thought. I could see his package beneath the thin film of the underwear, pressing against the cloth. And what a package it was: it hung low, barely contained by the underwear. I could just make out the tip of his cock there.

"Like what you see?" He asked, cockily.

I played it cool, shrugging. "Just wondering why a grown man wears tighty-whities, is all," I said. I tore my eyes away from his drooping cock, stopped myself from wondering what it looked like rock hard. "Maybe I'll call you that from now on: Tighty-whities."

He frowned, stepping awkwardly out of the pants around his ankles. I stared at the curves of powerful muscle in his legs, watched his obliques clench as he bent and tossed the pants towards me.

"Here. A souvenir," he said.

I gathered up his clothes with one hand, keeping the pistol pointed at him.

"Well, I've got to be going — but enjoy the amenities, gentlemen," I said, smirking.

I stepped towards the door ready to lock them in. Hot Cop stared at me with hatred in his eyes.

Then, a flash. It happened in an instant, when I took my eyes off of him for a mere moment. Grayson, who had been laying on the ground, shifted into his cat form: a miniature mountain lion. His paws slipped effortlessly out of my knots. He yowled and sprinted past me, over my feet and through the bars of the cells. *Hm. Guess I didn't think of that. Cat shifting might be more useful than I thought.*

But the distraction worked. I turned back towards the naked guy in front of me, but it was too late.

Hot Cop vanished into a flurry of fur and movement. He moved faster than any man — or Shifter — I'd ever seen.

Suddenly, I was thrown against the bars of the cell. The gun clattered to the floor, falling out of my grip.

Hot Cop reappeared inches away from my face, his sharp

features pressed to mine. His hand was around my throat — no, not hand. Claw. His forearm and hand had morphed into his half-wolf form. His fur was silvery-grey, claws black against my throat. His arm was wrapped in muscle, tensed at it held me firm against the wall.

And his near-naked body was pressed to mine. I could feel the warmth of his hard muscles pressed against my breasts, his muscular thighs almost wrapped around me as he held me in place. His mouth was so close to mine, and I looked at his soft, sensual lips, a perfect brown-pink beneath his beard. I felt his hot breath on me, smelling of peppermint and coffee. And the scent of his body, of his arms and armpits, almost overpowering. The musk of man just barely covered with deodorant. His scent alone made my pussy slick over with pleasure, and I could feel my magic pulse at his presence.

His eyes went wide; pupils dilating like dark beads. I stared into them, squirming under the grip of his claw. I gasped for breath, my lips still inches from his. Then, I felt it. His underwear against my bare thigh, beneath the running shorts, which had ridden up as he pressed me against the wall.

He's hard, I thought, and my groin ached at the thought. I could feel his cock pressing against his underwear, against my smooth leg. Feel the warm weight of it, so close to my clit, to my wet hole. *Fuck, I want it inside me,* I thought.

He stared at me, sudden confusion in his eyes. He leaned forward, smelled my hair deeply, and I saw something... *animal* cross his face. A snarl. His eyes flashed golden for a second, and the fur on his forearm rippled. His cock grew even more hard, and he pushed it forward, grinding it against my leg.

He feels it too, I thought.

Then he closed his eyes, shook the strange look away. The fur on his arm vanished, his claws turning into the firm grip of a man.

"The gun wasn't the most dangerous thing on me," he growled in my ear, "sweetheart."

He flipped me around, slamming my face into the bars.

Then I felt cold metal press onto my wrists, heard the sound of a lock clicking.

"What are you doing?" I asked, "get off of me!"

"Faerune cuffs," he said, "no magic for you outside, either. We're going to see the Mayor."

CHAPTER 4

Tighty-whities marched me out of the cell and into the police station. We moved down the hall, past one more cell, which sat empty, and a break room with a shitty coffee machine. He held my chains in one hand and his discarded clothes in another. Even outside the cell, I could feel the faerune cuffs sapping my magic. Iron would do that to a witch, especially when bewitched with extra wards. So long as those bracers were on my arms, painfully binding them behind my back, I was powerless.

"Stay still," Hot Cop said, pressing me against a wall. He released my cuffs, stepped backwards, and I heard the shuffle of fabric. I peered over my shoulder, watching his perfect ass disappear under his slacks. *A damn shame,* I thought. He pulled his shirt on, his muscles arching and flexing in a way that was painfully sexy. *What happened back there? I was ready to let him fuck me against those iron bars.*

I could tell he was uncomfortable about it, too. It wasn't a good look, being a cop getting hard around a delinquent. *Maybe I can use this to my advantage,* I thought.

When he was finished getting dressed, he led me outside. Instantly, cold spring air rushed over me. It felt heavenly. I breathed deep, savoring the water in the wind. It called to me, even bound by magic-dampening handcuffs.

The parking lot of the police station faced a tall stand

of pine trees. The sky was blue, dappled with grey and white clouds. From the position of the sun, which was behind us, casting shadows over the woods, I gathered it was the afternoon. A lone squad car stood in the parking lot, parked haphazardly over ancient looking asphalt. It was vintage, black and white with a golden crest that read: *Myston Sheriff.*

"Myston, huh," I said, "never heard of it. You guys like a cult or something? Some kind of Waco situation?"

Hot Cop said nothing. Instead, he led me down the concrete steps and towards the car. He put a hand on the back of my head and gingerly led me inside. I shivered at his touch on my hair, remembering his scent. I wanted those hands in my hair, pulling it, taking me for his needs…

Cool it. Clear your head.

I plopped into the back of the squad car. He climbed up front and started the engine.

"So… going to see the Mayor, huh," I said, "I know I deserve it, but I didn't think I'd get the key to the city just yet."

Again, no laughter. Only burning hot shame, radiating from the front seat. I sighed, leaned my head against the window. "My comedy is wasted in this town. I should go to New York," I said.

The squad car pulled out of the police station and on to the Main Street. The town was as small and idyllic as one could imagine: little houses painted bright colors, with wooden walls and Queen Anne sensibilities. Kids rode bikes on the street, waving to Hot Cop as he passed. Trees towered over the town, ancient and humbling in their size, fed by the nourishing waters of the lake. The neighborhood fell behind us and we came upon shops in a historic downtown: a book shop and a coffee shop, an antique store and a bank. Hot Cop parked next to the biggest building in town, a white church at the crossroads. The steeple towered over the small town, topped by a white cross.

"We're going to church? I'm not ready to say I do just yet, Tighty," I said.

He sighed. "God forbid. My mother would hate you," he

said. He got out of the car and pulled her out of the back seat. The town was sleepy, but a few cars and people moved about the street.

"We'll see the Mayor in a bit. First, coffee," he said.

"Now you're speaking my language," I said.

He guided me across the street, stopping to let a car pass, placing a hand in front of me. *A gentleman even to his prisoner,* I thought.

A small diner sat across the street from the church. The neon sign said "Lilith's." It looked straight out of 1950, with red, curved siding like a Cadillac. We stepped past the empty picnic tables outside and entered. A bell above the door rang as we walked inside.

"Lil?" Hot Cop called.

An older woman stepped out from the kitchen, wringing her hands on a wash cloth.

"Ace! Good to see you. The usual?"

She stopped in her tracks, her smile fading when she saw me. Her eyes flashed to my faerune cuffs, and I gave her a grin and little wiggle of my hands.

"And something for the lady," she said, shaking her head. "What have you done now, boy?" She asked.

Hot Cop — Ace, I guessed, which seemed like a stupid name — rolled his eyes. "I didn't do anything. She's just visiting, and has to answer a few questions."

She looked me up and down again. She was pretty, mid fifties, with grey-red hair and a motherly look about her. "Sure she is," she said, "I'll get the coffee." Then she disappeared behind the double doors into the kitchen. Ace led to me a booth with red vinyl seats and sat me down. Then he sat across from me, taking off his hat and rumpling his hair. He looked cute, in that lighting — casual. Not the intense sexual presence I'd felt in the cell, but something softer. Hot dad vibes.

"I thought you said your mom would hate me," I said, nodding my head towards Lilith and the kitchen.

He looked confused, then laughed. "She's not my mom.

Well, kind of. She's everybody's mom. She's been running this diner forever. Used to give me food even when I couldn't pay."

"That's cute," I said, "you're a softie, huh."

"Am I?" He said, and his eyes flashed golden again. Wolf eyes.

"Partial shifting. That's a pretty neat trick. And you're fast, too — I'd bet you're an Alpha, and a pretty powerful one," she said.

He shrugged. "I try and stay humble. How do you know so much about shifters, anyway?"

"You meet a lot of strange people, living on the streets. Especially if you're selling magic for money," I said.

"Ah. Wand for hire, huh. I guess I could have called it," he said. "How long have you been living rough?"

I thought for a moment. Did I really want to share this with him? But something about his demeanor, and the energy in the diner, made me comfortable. "Since my parents died."

"When was that?"

"When I was ten," I said.

He looked at me, then whistled. "And you've been on the road since then," he said.

I shrugged. "More or less. Did the system for a while. Didn't fit. Most families don't want a damaged girl for a daughter," I said.

"What makes you so damaged?" He asked.

"You watch your parents die, and tell me if you walk away fine upstairs," I said. I tapped my temple.

He was about to speak, mouth hanging open in shock, when Lilith came out of the kitchen. She pressed the double doors open with her butt and came out carrying a tray of food and coffee. "You hoo!" She called, "Order up!"

The cheery tone ground awkwardly against our previous conversation. Lilith leaned over the table, putting a coffee in front of both of us. "Two creams, two sugars for you, Ace," she said. She placed a black coffee in front of me, "didn't know how you wanted yours, so I brought everything. Toast and jam for both of you, eggs and pancakes coming right up, sweetie."

She smiled at the Sheriff and at me, then backed away. Ace gave a big smile back, then sipped his coffee.

"Two creams, two sugars?" I asked.

He paused over his cup. "Yeah? So?"

"That's the tighty-whities of coffee orders," I said.

He grinned over his coffee, "classic and beloved by all?" He said.

"Little kid shit," she said.

"Big words coming from the street rat. What are you, seventeen?"

"Twenty one," I said, "what are you, forty?"

He scowled. "Twenty eight," he said, "and what's your coffee order, big girl?"

"Black," she said, "the way it was meant to be enjoyed." I left out the part where I could rarely get my hands on coffee anyways.

"Of course. People who take their coffee black have trust issues," he said.

I blabbered. "How could you possibly come to that conclusion?"

He smirked. "Afraid to look indulgent. Afraid to look weak. People who need to feel strong all the time are people who can't trust others to have their backs," he said.

I leaned back, looked out the window. "That's ridiculous," I said.

"Says the girl who wouldn't let Grayson change her bandages," he said.

I scowled. "You know, it would be a lot easier to drink this coffee if I didn't have these cuffs on. What are you going to do, spoon feed me?"

"Hm. As humiliating as that would be for you — no. And maybe you'd be less annoying with something in your mouth," he said.

My face went sheet white. He froze too, realizing what he'd said. I remembered his cock pressed against my leg and felt my groin squirm, my magic trying to call out to him.

"I mean—" he started.

"Pancakes," I said, "in my mouth, I got it. And sausage, too, I guess."

He spat out his coffee.

* * *

He stood and unlocked one half of the cuffs, bringing around my other arm so that he could cuff them in front of me. I looked to the exit, wondering if I could sneak in a cheap shot, if my magic would work with only one cuff on —

"Don't try anything stupid," he said, "I'm faster than you are, even without shifting."

I knew he was right. Instead, I let him re-cuff me and lower me back into the seat. I grabbed the coffee with my cuffed hands and savored the warmth of the mug, the smell of the grounds. Steam lifted off the chipped ceramic, floating upwards in the afternoon sun. I smelled it, sipped. It was heaven after the shitty break-room coffee from the station.

"That's better," I said, almost orgasmically, "so much better."

Lilith brought the pancakes and eggs, and Ace started wolfing them down — quite literally, I guess. I did too, and soon my stomach was full to bursting. Once my plate was clear, I leaned back and started my second cup of coffee.

"So what is this place? Some kind of shifter town?" I said.

He looked up from his plate. "Yeah. And more. We take all types, but a lot of us are shifters or family. And a few other, rarer kinds of folk. But everyone mostly keeps a low profile. We like it that way."

"Huh. Whole town run by shifters," I said. I'd heard rumors of such things existing, but their locations were usually secret. "Must be a handful to be the sheriff," I said.

He exhaled. "You don't know the half of it. But usually it's a drunk bear shifter falling asleep in the street, or breaking into the grocery store. At least, up until recently."

"What happened recently?" I asked, curious.

"You," he said. He looked at me sternly.

"Me? Why me? You guys don't ever get new people in town?" I said.

"Not really, no, except for tourists.. The whole island is warded. Ancient magic, going back to the Dawn Days. That's why we settled here. No one is supposed to just float past the wards and wind up on the beach."

"Maybe your wards just suck," I said.

He shook his head. "You don't get it. This is fae-magic. No one — not even a powerful witch — should be able to break it."

I frowned. I'd always had raw power, if I lacked polish. But if what he was saying was true, there was no way I could have washed up ashore. Especially if I wasn't even conscious at the time. *Good news is, I should be safe here. At least for a while. If these wards are fae-magic, not even the One Eyed Wolf should be able to get through.* I relaxed a little at the thought. At least that was one problem put aside; now I just needed to figure out what to do about Hot Cop and his little town of shifters.

"If I'm such a problem, why not just put me on a boat out of here? I won't tell anyone you're here. Even if I did, who would believe me?"

"It's more complicated than that. We're a real town, in the mortal world, too. There's a bridge that connects us to the mainland. But the bridge is the only way on or off the island; it's a gate in the wards. We can usually control who comes in or out, though, and we always know when they come. Except for you."

"So what now?" I asked.

He exhaled. "Now the Mayor," he said, "we need someone smarter than I am."

"Why should I trust him? Or you, for that matter?" I asked.

He sighed. "Black coffee," he said.

"Oh shut up."

* * *

Ace left a wad of cash on the table and then stood up to find Lilith. He took me with, but told me to wait outside the kitchen door. "If you run, I'll know," he said. Then he smiled and pointed to his nose, then to his ears. *Shifter senses,* I thought.

He went into the kitchen, and I heard soft voices. I looked at the door, briefly contemplating making a break for it, only to decide not to. I had no idea how to get the faerune cuffs off, anyway. There was no way I was getting off the island without magic. Instead, I stepped towards the kitchen door and pressed my ear against it.

Hushed voices came from other side.

"What did it say?" Ace asked, quietly.

"It's confusing," said Lilith, "I've never seen grounds like this. Look at these patterns. Spirals, nearly perfect. Her power is huge. She's no ordinary witch, Ace."

"Let me see," he said. "You got all that from this?"

"The grounds don't lie. Better than tea leaves, anyhow. I'm telling you, Ace: that girl is trouble."

Divination with coffee grounds, I thought, *that's a new one. Must be a witch too, or a psychic.*

I closed my eyes, summoning my second sight. When I opened them, the diner reappeared in lines of bright blue. Through the wall, I could see Ace and Lilith standing by the coffee machine. Ace held a coffee cup, looking at the grounds there. I was right; there was some divination magic lingering around the cup. I could see Ace and his wolf spirit standing there, and see Lilith next to him. But nothing seemed off about her — there was no swell of magical light that might indicate a witch.

But she turned to the door, as if sensing my eyes on her.

"You better go," she said, "your friend is getting restless."

Ace turned, looking at the door. I shut off my second sight and the wall reappeared, solid and white. I stepped back from the door just as Ace opened it. He looked at me, suspicious.

"Ready?" I asked, with my most innocent smile.

He grabbed me by the wrist and led me to the door. But I felt Lilith's eyes lingering on me as I left. *Something's up in this town,* I thought, *I can feel it.*

As the sheriff took me out the front door, I turned to see

Lilith standing there, watching me, a frown on her face.

CHAPTER 5

I thought we'd go across the street to the church, but Ace put me back in the squad car. We pulled out of the diner's parking lot and rode slowly along the Main Street, towards the edge of town. We passed fish markets and a quaint grocery store, and little lakeside restaurants and houses. The lake swelled over the horizon, huge and bright blue today. The shore here was sandy, not stony, and boat docks jutted out into the bay. White fishing boats and sail boats bobbed in the harbor.

Ace picked up the road that went along the side of the lake, and we left the town, heading into the forest.

"How big is this island?" I asked.

He shrugged. "That's complicated."

"Magic?"

"Magic. But there's a few villages on it that stick around most of the time. Myston is the biggest," he said.

"Myston... Texas?" I said.

He grinned.

"Myston, Minnesota. That's Lake Superior," he said.

Minnesota confirmed. What is that, six hours from Minneapolis to Chicago? A day or two of hitching it. Seems like we're farther north than that, though, almost up towards Canada. It'll be a bitch getting out of here.

We drive along the lakeshore for a while until the road took us inland. Towering pine trees covered the road, which quickly turned into dirt.

"Mayor lives all the way out here?" I asked.

"Likes privacy," he said, looking at me through the mirror.

In the split second that he looked at me through the mirror, something crashed onto the hood on the car.

The world erupted into chaos.

I could hear crunching metal and shattering glass, and the whole world shook.

Ace shouted something, but I couldn't hear him over the roar of the broken engine.

I opened my eyes. On the hood of the car, crouched, was a man. Around him, the hood of the squad car had crushed like paper. The windshield was cracked, the airbags deployed. I'd smacked my head on the glass divider in front of me, and blood dripped into my eyes. The wound in my stomach screamed as the stitches came undone.

The man on the hood looked up. He had white hair, paper white skin, and blood red eyes. The irises gleamed like rubies in the daylight. He wore black leather: a black leather duster, black leather pants, black leather gloves. His shirt was black cotton. Around his throat, an amulet gleamed: ruby set in gold.

Vampire.

He smirked and punched through the glass windshield, grabbing Ace by the throat. I screamed as the vampire tore Ace from the squad car, throwing him through the air. Ace sailed out of sight, into the woods. The vampire turned back towards me. His movements were inhumanly quick; as he struck, his limbs blurred.

Suddenly, he was outside the squad car, standing next to the door. He grabbed the handle and ripped the door off its hinges, sending it sailing into the woods. The scream of metal made my ears ring.

He crouched, looking in at me, cowering in the back seat.

"Anastasia Walker," he said, "there's been a change of plans. You're coming with me"

"Like hell I am," I said, but my voice shook. He rolled his

eyes and started crawling into the back seat, grabbing at my legs. I kicked him square in the jaw.

It was like kicking stone.

He only smiled.

"Hurt your foot, didn't it," he said.

"Yeah," I grumbled, "a little."

Then he grabbed my ankle and started pulling me out of the back seat. I screamed and thrashed, but I might as well have been a child. He pulled me out of the car and I thudded to the ground. The wind left my lungs, and I gasped painfully. He began to drag me across the dirt road, then through pine needles on the forest floor. A black motorcycle waited for us, concealed behind pine trees.

"Where are you taking me?" I screamed, trying to grab onto anything I could.

"Nothing personal. Boss's orders," he said.

Suddenly, a snarl from our right. The vampire turned just in time to see a massive silver wolf crash into his side. He raised his arms and I watched as Ace's wolf form clamped down on his forearm. The force of the hit drove the vampire back into the bushes. Ace's wolf form looked down at me. "Are you alright?" It said. I always hated when shifters talked in their animal forms. It made me feel like I was in a bad kid's movie with talking animals.

"Fine, he only — look out!" I screamed. The vampire blurred past me, colliding with Ace. They disappeared in a tumble of blurring movements, snarling teeth and fur and black leather. I backed up, checking myself. No horrible injuries, but blood was seeping through my shirt where my bullet wound had burst the stitches.

I ran back towards the car, faerune cuffs clinking noisily. I might have been magic-less, but I wasn't defenseless. I climbed into the ruined driver's seat and found Ace's pistol waiting there. I took it, turned off the safety, and cocked it. Then I ran back to where Ace and the vampire battled beneath the pines.

I aimed the gun, but they moved too fast. If I fired, I'd have an equal shot of hitting Ace. Not that I thought a bullet would really kill a vampire — I wasn't that naive — but it might slow him down.

"Ace!" I called, "Separate!"

He must have heard me, because the blur of fur and teeth became two separate forms. Ace looked battered, with bloody wounds covering his body. The vampire's clothes were scratched, but he looked nearly unscathed.

I took aim and fired, aiming right between the creature's eyes.

The bastard didn't even try to move. He let the bullet hit him in the forehead. The force knocked his head backwards, but that was all. He looked at me, smiling, the only proof he'd been struck being a thin spread of cracks on his skin.

"Stoneskin Clan," Ace's wolf form growled, "put it away, Ana. We won't win this fight."

Ace turned back to the vampire. "What do you want with her?" He asked.

The vampire smiled. I could see sharp teeth stretching over his full, red lips. "She is the Vessel."

"Vessel?" I asked.

The vampire turned to look at me. "Don't play coy. I've been paid a small treasure to retrieve you, so that my employer can... well, you will see."

He seemed to purr the words.

"I don't know about any Vessel," I said, "I'm a nobody. I promise."

He shrugged, then sighed. "Fine. Have it your way." He stepped towards me.

"Wait!" I said, "if you're only in it for the money, maybe we can come to some sort of arrangement."

He smiled. "I said I'm being paid a small treasure. Not all treasure is kept in banks, darling," he said.

I looked to Ace, who growled, stepping towards the vampire.

The vampire flashed, blurring towards me. I dropped

to the ground, cowering. He came within inches before Ace sideswiped him, jaws clamping onto his face. The two disappeared, battling again, a blur of leather and fur.

Ace can't take much more, I thought. I opened my eyes, only to see the remains of Ace's police uniform next to me: tattered shreds of blue pants, shirt, and jacket, torn up when Ace had shifted. And in the middle, the vaporized remains of tighty-whities. And inside them, the gleam of silver.

My eyes widened. I crawled towards it.

In the heap of fabric was Ace's key ring. And on it, a small silver key, arced with faerunes. The key to my handcuffs. I scrambled for it, carefully putting it into position. It clicked into place, and I had to turn it with my teeth. The faerune cuffs clicked open and fell to the forest floor.

Magic washed over me.

I felt it rising like a tidal wave. Like a siren's song.

Behind me, a crash.

The vampire whipped Ace into a tree, shattering the wood. Ace landed thirty feet away, skidding to a stop, pushing up a mound of dirt like he was a meteorite fallen to earth. I watched as he lost consciousness, his wolf form shifting back to his human form, beaten and broken.

The vampire smirked, victorious.

"Hey babe," I said, calling over to him. He looked at me, eyes wide when he saw my hands were free, "change of plans," I said.

I raised my hands, calling up my magic. I reached into the water in the air, into the water in the soil, even the water in the pine trees. All around us, they blackened and shriveled and fell, and water rose from them, like souls from corpses. I raised my hands above my head, and the water rose like tentacles. I stood in the center of a battle arrangement like a giant squid.

The vampire's mouth dropped open.

I reached out with a tentacle of water as thick as a man, and wrapped it around the vampire's torso. He struggled against it, but he was no match for the rush of my current. Vampires, after all, can't cross running water.

I moved my hands around my head, working the water whip. It reared back, and like an arm, threw the vampire through the air.

He soared, vanishing over the tree tops, far, far away from us.

My magic hummed for one more moment, and then vanished, depleted. And with it gone, my strength fled. I fell to the ground unconscious.

CHAPTER 6

"Ana? Ana!" The grey fog faded and I awoke, my eyes fluttering open. Ace stood above me, battered and bruised, a concerned look on his sexy-ass face.

And he was naked.

Totally, completely naked.

For a moment, in my dazed state, I let my eyes wash dreamily over his muscular body: his two brown nipples, his hairy stomach, his adonis belt, his—

Oh. *Oh.*

I shuffled back, coming to my senses, trying not to look at his cock. It hung between his legs, proud and girthy, thick even while soft. And it was huge. *Maybe you'd be less annoying with something in your mouth.* Hell, maybe I would.

He looked concerned. "Ana, are you alright?" He said.

I tore my eyes away from his perfect cock, but found only his perfect face. My groin throbbed just looking at him, my clit sparking to life. I tried to look at something else, and instead found the cross tattooed on his right chest.

"What the fuck was that?" I asked.

"Bounty hunter, looks like," he said.

"A vampire bounty hunter? You usually have these on your island?"

He shook his head. "This would be a first. Vamps can't cross running water without help. Someone must have let him over the bridge."

"That means…" I said.

"Someone on the island is out to get you? Yeah," he said.

Fuck.

He stepped towards me, and I saw the curve of the muscles in his thigh, his juicy ass shaking with each step. He was built like a professional baseball player, all testosterone. Not a pretty boy, but a man who would take you out to dinner and then call you a dirty little slut in bed. Pull your hair and eat your wet…

Cool it, Walker.

"Could you — you know…" I nodded down towards his exposed genitals.

"Oh — oh, right. Uh — my clothes kind of exploded. Let me check the car," he said. He moved towards the ruined squad car, and I watched his ass flex as he walked away. I cocked my head, admiring the little patch of dark hair he had just above the crack, but how smooth the cheeks were. I imagined my fingernails digging into those cheeks as he thrust inside me.

Why does mortal peril make me so horny? I thought.

He came back from the squad car with an old pair of jeans slipped on. They hung low, just exposing the tip of his pubes over the waistband. His adonis belt pointed like a V towards the zipper, and his stomach heaved as he breathed heavily. *Not much better,* I thought.

"Sorry," he said, "no shirt."

"Of course," I said.

"You're bleeding pretty bad," he said. He nodded to my torso. Blood spread across the white t-shirt from my bullet wound. *Stitches. Fuck.* I looked at him; bite and slash marks covered his body, along with deep blue bruises. "You too," I said, "here."

I stepped towards him. He tensed as I grew near. *Probably afraid of whatever happened last time we got this close.*

As I stepped towards him, I smelled him again. This time it was pine needles, sweat, and dirty skin. It was stunningly sexy, but I put a damper on it. I reached out to a slash in his side and let my hand hover above it. Then I closed my eyes and reached inside for my magic. It was weak now, after what I'd done with the water whip. But it was just enough: I reached out for water in the air, for water in his blood. And, summoning my power, I sealed the gash closed.

He breathed deeply as the gash vanished, glowing water flowing through the cut. I did another, and he winced again. By the time I got to the third cut, my magic was completely dry. "That's it," I said, "I'm out."

"You haven't healed yourself," he said.

"I can't. Witches can't heal themselves, only others," I said.

He frowned. "Thank you. For healing me," he said. It was then, with the deep closeness of his voice, that I realized we were still standing chest to chest. My hand rested on his abs, where his wound had been.

"I—"

"Ace!" A voice came.

We both turned. A beautiful woman with bright red hair ran into the clearing. She wore a simple flannel and blue jeans, and her face was taught with worry.

Ace backed away from, red faced. He stepped towards the woman, enveloping her in an embrace. He nuzzled his face in her hair and kissed her cheek. I saw the woman's golden eyes staring at me over Ace's muscled shoulders.

"Ace, who is this?" She asked.

Ace turned to me. "Tara, this is Ana. Ana, this is Tara, the Mayor. My mate."

CHAPTER 7

"What happened?" Tara asked, looking over at the ruined squad car. "Vampire," Ace breathed.

"On the island? How?" Tara asked.

He shrugged. "No idea. Someone must have helped him cross the bridge," he said.

Tara shook her head. "That makes no sense. Why would someone on the Isle do that?"

Ace looked over his shoulder at me. "He was after her," he said.

Tara appraised me with golden eyes. "And who is she?" She asked.

"Nobody," I said, "in fact, I was just leaving."

Ace stepped towards me: "Whoah, whoah. What do you mean?"

I raised my hands. "No shackles now, remember?"

Ace frowned. 'And just when I thought we were getting along," he said.

"Don't kid yourself. I was a prisoner," I said.

"We just need to figure out what's going on — then you can go," he said, "I promise." He reached out a hand to me like I was a scared animal.

I shook my head. "I don't trust people, remember? You're included in that. So if you're done, I'm going to leave."

"This is ridiculous," mumbled Tara.

Ace held up his other hand to soothe her. *Am I crazy? I thought, he was going wild for me. And he was flirting back. When he pushed me up against that wall, I felt something I've never felt before. But now he has a mate? And if I know anything, it's that shifters mate for life.*

Ace's eyes narrowed. "You said it yourself, Ana — you're out of magic. You just used it all."

I rolled my eyes. "Yeah, healing *you* — doesn't that earn me a little something? Like freedom?"

"I'm sorry but I can't do that. I have a duty to the people on this island," he said.

"Yeah, well, I don't. So I'm gonna go now," she said.

"I'm faster than you, and you don't have any spells," he said, stepping forward.

I took the pistol from my waistband. "I actually have one spell. It's called 'gun.'"

Ace's face dropped. A bullet wouldn't kill him unless I got him through the brain, and even then it was iffy, depending on how powerful he was. But it would slow him down either way. I wasn't exactly a crack shot, but he didn't need to know that — I'd gotten lucky with the vamp, so he probably thought I was American Sniper or something.

"Maybe we can talk this out..." he started, grinning nervously.

"Oh my god, move," Tara said. She pushed him aside and stepped forward. "Kid time is over," she said. Then she raised her hands, and fire began to crackle at her fingertips.

Shit. Flame witch, I thought. I raised the gun, but it was too late.

She pushed her magic outward, and the flames tightening into ropes that wrapped around my hands. She controlled the flame ropes with her mind and bound me there, unable to move. Fire tinged the hair on my hands, and I dropped the pistol to the floor.

"Never send a wolf to do a witch's job," Tara said, putting

one hand on her hip.

* * *

Ace cuffed me, and Tara released her flame-rope spell. *That's pretty tricky magic, binding me without burning me. She must be powerful.* Ace led me through the woods, along the dirt road, leaving the ruined cruiser behind. He and Tara bickered the whole way.

Tara lived in a cabin in the woods, far outside of town; cute wooden walls, rustic kitchen, cast iron pots hanging from hooks. She went into the basement and got a first aid kit, then started stitching us up.

"Vampire bounty hunter? On the island?" She asked.

"Stoneskin Clan," Ace said, "a bullet didn't do anything but scratch him."

"Well that's a problem," Tara said, cocking her head.

"Understatement of the eon," Ace said.

"What was he after?" Tara asked. She poured herself a mug of tea, warming it with glowing red hands.

Ace looked at me. "Her," he said.

"And who is she?" Tara asked, nodding towards me.

"Um, someone who is right here?" I said.

Tara smiled flatly. "Right. Sorry. Who are *you,*" she said.

"None of your god damn business," I said.

Tara rolled her eyes and raised her hands in exasperation. She looked to Ace, but he just shrugged.

"She washed up on shore last night," Ace said, "water witch, from the looks of it. Somehow got through the wards."

Tara arched an eyebrow. She had pretty eyebrows, well kept and manicured. Everything about her was well-kept, in a rustic sort of way. Tight body, toned like a track runner. Perfectly voluminous red hair. Bright golden eyes set in a face without much makeup. She was the perfect down-home girl for Ace's hometown hunk. She probably even knew how to cook.

"That's not possible," she said, "those wards are faerie magic."

"Tell it to her," Ace said.

Tara stepped over to me, appraising me with shrewd eyes. She pursed her lips, the grabbed my chin with her face. She looked deeply into my eyes.

"Hey, hands off!" I said, jerking away. She held my face tightly.

"Pretty little thing, huh," she said, more to herself than anyone else. Ace shifted uncomfortably.

"I... I guess," he said, looking away.

"You take her to Lil?" She asked, still gazing into my eyes.

"Yeah," he said.

"What did she say?" Tara asked.

"It's... complicated. We can talk later," he said.

Tara lifted my face in her hand and then shrugged. "Hm," she said. Then her fingers closed around a single thread of my hair, and yanked it.

"Ow!" I shouted, "what the fuck?"

She ignored me, staring at the strand of hair. She moved to the corner of the room, where a fire crackled in the river-stone hearth.

She tossed the flame in and watched it crackle, her eyes flashing gold as she stared, reading whatever she saw in the flames. *Scrying with fire. I've never seen a witch do that before.*

"Powerful..." she murmured, "a dark fate ahead of her. And a man... shrouded in shadow. That's all I can see."

She stood, frowning. "What is your name, girl?"

"Ana," Ace said, before I could speak.

"Full name," she said.

"None of your—"

"Damn business, yeah, we get it. Believe it or not, kid, we're trying to help you. We can't do that if you keep being a little asshole," Tara said. She stood with her arms folded.

I frowned, looking between them. *Black coffee,* I thought.

"Anastasia. Anastasia Walker," I said.

She thought for a moment, lips moving. "I don't know any Walker witches. What coven are you from?"

I shook my head, "Loner. No coven."

"Hedge witch. Okay. What about your parents? Mom have a coven?" She said.

"No clue. We lived in Pennsylvania though," I said.

She nodded, then moved to the bookshelf in the living room. She took down a book the size of a human torso and put in on the kitchen table. The old wood plumed with dust as she did. She began flipping through the pages.

"West... Wu... Winegard... Wallas...Walking Bear... No Walker family in here. Dad was a mortal?" She asked.

I nodded. "Orthodontist," I said.

"Could be the Philly coven," Ace said, stepping forward.

"Unlikely," said Tara, "they're pretty good about record keeping. Wouldn't surprise me with Briar Hill, though. Their secretary is awful."

She slammed the book shut, then leaned on the table, exhausted.

"Your mom ever mention anything about your bloodline? Ancestors?" She said.

I shook my head. "Nah. She was pretty quiet about the witch stuff. I figured out most of what I know on my own."

She raised an eyebrow again. "Self taught?" She said, looking to Ace.

He nodded, eyes wide. "And she threw that vamp half a mile out into the lake."

Tara appraised me again. "A hedge witch from nowhere with incredible power. A vampire bounty hunter stalking her. What else is new?"

"You forgot the werewolf pack that wants me dead," I said, "how I got into this whole mess."

"A pack? Which pack?" She said.

I shrugged. "Dunno. Their leader was a big white wolf with one eye, though," I said, casually.

Both Ace and Tara's eyes widened in shock. Ace's mouth hung open.

"You didn't tell me that!" He hissed.

I blinked. "What?"

"That you were being hunted by... that it was..." Ace couldn't finish the sentence.

Tara looked at him, closing her eyes. "You didn't think this would be important to figure out?"

He raised his hands defensively. "We thought it was Duluth! Or Voyager Pack, maybe! Not fucking.... fucking...."

"Fucking *what?*" I screamed, exhausted.

Ace and Tara shared another look.

"Ogen One-Eye," Ace said, "the banished Shifter King."

CHAPTER 8

"So he's the King," I said, "who cares?"

Tara rolled her eyes. "You wouldn't get it," she said, "you're just a kid."

My eyes narrowed at that. "And you're just an old lady, so. Here we are."

Her mouth dropped open. "I'm thirty," she said.

"And he's twenty eight… robbing the cradle a little bit, huh."

"You know, you don't need to be annoying just for the sake of it. You can think before you speak. Really make the insults count," she said.

I stuck out my tongue and made a farting noise. Tara pinched the bridge of her nose. "I'm gonna kill her," she said.

Ace stepped forward, diffusing the situation.

"Not just the King," Ace said, "he's kind of like a god. A legend. He was the first Viking shifter that came to North America and united the shifter clans here. Then he gathered up more power, magical knowledge, and ruled the North American Underworld for centuries."

"Then what happened?" I asked.

"About a hundred years ago, they banished him to the

Fae," he said.

I looked at him, then at Tara.

Then I started laughing.

"You're joking," I said, "that was a good one."

"What?" Ace said.

"The Fae? Fairyland? Come on," I said.

Tara looked at me like I was a worm in her apple. "Oh my god. She really doesn't know anything," she said.

Ace shook his hands in front of his face. "Wait, wait. So you're telling me that you, a witch, is standing with us, a werewolf and a witch, and we just got attacked by a vampire… but you draw the line at fairies?"

I shrugged. "Yeah, pretty much," I said. People on the road talked about the Fae sometimes, but they were usually crackpots. On drugs or something. Once, someone had tried to approach me to open a portal to the Fae. I basically told him not to call me again. And of course everyone knew about faerunes, but that didn't mean fairies were real. They were supposed to be myths.

Tara exhaled. "We don't have time for this," she said, "how do we even know she's telling the truth? About One Eye?"

Ace folded his hands over his broad chest. "Why wouldn't she? She's got no reason to lie. Besides, it seems like she doesn't even know who One Eye is."

I raised my manacled hands. "Got me," I said.

"Shit. Shit shit shit," Tara said.

"What's so bad about him?" I asked, "Why'd he get banished in the first place?"

Ace sighed. "He didn't become the Were King with rainbows and cupcakes. He did it with blood and magic. If he's back, he won't be satisfied living in the shadows. He'll come for us. For the whole Underworld."

"Okay, but what does he want with me?" I asked, "like you said, I'm nobody."

Tara pressed off the counter, put her hands on it to steady herself. "Clearly not, if the Lost King is tracking you. There must be something else going on.”

“Think he sent the vamp?” Ace aced Tara.

She shook her head. “Ogen was — is — a shifter supremacist. He’ll tolerate magicians because he needs us, but he despises vampires. He’s the one that caused all the old clan wars. No way he’d hire one, instead of sending some of his own.”

“Which means….” I said.

“Which means he’s not the only one after you. Someone else is, someone with money and power to buy a vamp bounty hunter,” Tara said.

I thought for a moment, contemplating. Then I said: “There’s something else. The vamp that ambushed us — he called me a Vessel.”

Tara’s head snapped up. “A what?”

I shrugged. “Don’t know,” I said.

Ace’s face screwed up in concentration. “What, like a boat? A jar? What else could a Vessel be?”

Tara thought hard, her perfect eyebrows knitting together. “I don’t know,” she murmured, “whatever it is, it can’t be good. That could be why One Eye is after you, too. Think. Ana — has anyone ever called you a Vessel?”

I closed my eyes, thought. Nothing came to me. “I don’t know— maybe something a client said?” I sighed. “I’m lost.”

Tara pursed her lips. “Helpful,” she said, “so helpful.”

“Okay, smartass, you figure it out,” I said.

She looked at me with a withering glare. “You know, you’re really glib for someone being hunted by a semi-divine Wolf King and a vampire bounty hunter.”

“And you’re really stuck up for someone who says they’re trying to help,” I said.

“Nice girls don’t keep people alive,” she said.

Ace stepped in between us. “Okay ladies let’s simmer down. What we’ve discovered is that Ana, for whatever reason, is in danger. Despite the wards on the house, that means we’re all in danger. So what’s the plan?”

The room was silent for a minute. “As much as I hate to

admit it, we need to take her to Castle Rock," she said.

He blinked. "Really?"

"Where else has wards strong enough to keep out Ogen One-Eye? We'll keep here there until we figure out what's going on. Maybe she can learn to control her powers while she's there, too."

"Castle Rock?" I asked, "what's that?"

Ace looked to Tara, who nodded. "An old fort, built on a rock off the island. Kinda like a school, I guess."

"It's where we train the island's defenses. Get newbies up to speed," Tara said.

"Oh *hell* no," I said, standing, "no way you're sending me to school. I'm twenty-one fucking years old! And I haven't been in school since the eighth grade," I said.

Tara's eyes opened in mock surprise. "So that's why you're like this," she said. She dropped the act. "Relax. It's not homework. It's a place you can learn about magic, about our ways here on the island. And it's just until we figure out something to do with you."

Ace stepped up to me, put his big hands on my shoulders. I could see the setting sun on his crisp jaw line. "It's the safest place for you. Castle Rock has stronger wards than even the island. It's a fortress dating back to the Dawn Days," he said, "there's no safer place for you."

"Fine," I said, "just until we get these people off my back, explain it's a misunderstanding. Then I'm out of here. Got it?"

Ace looked relieved. "Got it," he said.

Tara stepped forward. Gingerly, she took Ace's hand off my shoulder.

"We can't leave tonight. It's already dark. Woods won't be safe," she said.

"Vamp?" I asked.

Ace considered. "And other stuff. Woods get pretty spooky on the island at night. Nothing gets in, but nothing gets out, either. And it's an old island, steeped in magic. We don't allow people in the woods at night."

"It's settled then. Babe, start dinner. I feel like I need a shower," Tara said. She gave me one last look before she went upstairs.

Some alpha, getting bossed around by his girlfriend. But I guess he's a good guy on top of everything.

Ace started cooking, tossing the dish rag over his shoulder. He wore a flannel he evidently kept at Tara's house, but he wore it open. *He sure does like having his shirt off,* I thought, *I guess I can see why. And he can cook. Fuck me, right?*

He brought me a glass of red wine as I sat on the couch, then poured one for himself. "Sorry about her," he said, "Tara can get... possessive."

Again, I can see why, I thought.

"What's her deal? When you said we were going to see the Mayor, I thought..."

"It would be a dude? Tsk, tsk. Some Gen Z you are," he said, smirking.

"I thought it wouldn't be your girlfriend. Mate. Whatever. I don't know how shifters work," I said.

"Mate, girlfriend... we aren't pack bonded yet, not until we have a kid," he said, "which she is very adamant about putting off."

"But you want them?" I asked, sipping my wine.

He smiled. "What's not to want? Little shifter babies running around underfoot?" He said.

"Doesn't she also have to be a shifter for you to mate?" I asked.

"She can flame shift," he said, "but she got her wolf form from me. She's pretty powerful."

Damn, I thought, *elemental shifting. That puts her on the level of Sorceress, not just witch.* I wondered if I could take her in a fight, if I had a full reserve of magic.

"My mom could water shift," I said, "she would turn into an otter. That was always fun, days at the lake," I said.

"And you? Any shifting?" He said. He seasoned the steak with salt, then pepper. It looked raw and bloody.

"No. I mean, I've never tried. I probably have the power, just not the precision," I said.

"Hoo hoo. So cocky," he said.

"That's not what I meant—"

"Don't be sorry," he said, "it's cute."

His face went white as soon as he said it. His lips pursed. "I mean— cute in a kid way. Like a little kid. Like a daughter," he said. It was like he vomited the words.

"Like a daughter," I said, tapping my lips, "okay, daddy."

He scowled. Then he looked upstairs and stepped towards me, slowly. He sat on the couch. "Listen… about what happened, back in the cell. That was an accident."

"Hm. You seemed like you were about to have an accident in your tighty-whities," I said.

"Shh! Look, Tara can never know. Nothing happened. It was my wolf, he… he felt something. I didn't. Okay?" He said.

I nodded, but part of me was disappointed. "Okay. Right. Nothing happened," I said. I didn't want to get in the way of anything. I wanted to get off the island, back to my normal life, sipping beer and selling spells.

He smiled a close lipped smile and then stood. He extended a hand to me. "Come on," he said, "I wanna show you something."

I took his hand cautiously, and he led me outside. We stepped onto the porch, silent except for the sound of creaking floorboards and crickets. The night air was cool, but I could smell woodsmoke from the stove and pine needles from the woods. In the distance, waves crashed against a rocky shore.

"What is it?" I asked.

He took me to the edge of the porch. "Look up," he said.

I did.

Above us, more stars than I had ever seen twinkled in an ink black sky. It was if the sky was a painting, one of bright white and blue and indigo, purple and yellow and green. In the distance, above the pine trees dipped in shadow, the aurora borealis hung like a luminescent river. My breath caught in my throat.

"Holy…" I started, but couldn't finish. The look of it almost brought tears to my eyes.

"I know, right," he said with a boyish grin, "the wards around the island keep out light, too, so there's zero light pollution. You're looking at what the stars on earth would look like if humanity never existed."

"It's beautiful," I said, whispering.

"I know," he said, but he was looking only at me.

CHAPTER 9

Dinner was steak with peppercorn sauce and red wine. I tore into like a dog, savoring every bloody bite. I never had the money for steak, but Ace explained that the cows were all raised on the island. Same with the vegetables. Something about the magic on the island made them grow strong and fast even in cold northern Minnesota. Tara didn't talk much during dinner, but Ace chattered happily, asking me questions. He'd been kind enough to — cautiously — remove my faerune cuffs so I could eat. Then he explained that he could leave them off.

"Try and run, and you won't make it out the woods alive," he said.

"Is that a threat?" I asked, arching in eyebrow.

"More like an honest warning. We've got monsters in these woods you've never even heard of," he said.

"Gotcha," I said, taking another bite of steak and then washing it down with red wine.

After dinner, we all did dishes. With my cuffs off, the washing part was easy. I washed every plate with a spray of water and soap, and Tara dried them all with fire. Then Ace put them away. Good team work, I thought.

When it came time for bed, Ace set me up with a pillow and comforter on the couch. The he went upstairs to be with his girlfriend.

The sounds of them fucking kept me up *all night*.

It was endless. Almost every half hour to start, and then every hour onward. Tara screamed and moaned, and the whole house shook with Ace's thrusts. *Don't you people sleep?* I thought, covering my head with a pillow. I could still hear Ace's groans through the fabric. He fucked her like an animal, always hungry for more. I heard every naughty word I knew come out of his mouth: *You're my dirty little slut,* he said, and: *are you going to take my cock, bitch? You like that?*

It made me helplessly wet.

Fuck, I thought, *he's a hot cop, he cooks steak for dinner, he has a god-like body, nice dad vibes but is also a Dom in bed?*

I groaned into my pillow, wishing for the night to be over.

Suddenly, the sounds of fucking stopped from upstairs.

"What was that?" Tara asked, distantly.

Shit. The cabin has thin walls, of course.

"I'll go check," came Ace's breathless voice.

I heard plodding down the cabin stairs, and I quickly closed my eyes, pulling my fingers away from myself.

I kept my eyes barely open, looking through my lashes. And there was Ace, standing over the living room, scanning for danger. Protecting me. He was naked, and still hard: I watched his massive cock swing as he walked towards me. It looked slick with something, and precum dribbled from the tip.

He panted, out of breath. He looked sweaty, chest heaving, as if he came back from a jog. At least he was working hard, I thought. To my surprise, he looked upstairs, then stepped over to me, apparently making sure I was okay. He whispered my name. "Ana," he said.

I pretended to be asleep, shutting my eyes tighter.

Then, I felt him lean close to me. I could feel his breath on my cheek, his musk and stink in the air next to me. My pussy started dripping again, and I struggled not to squirm.

Then I felt it; his finger, moving a stray hair from my face. Just so he could look at me better. Then a deep inhale, and his nose pressed against my hair. He was smelling me.

I can't tell if I should be creeped out, flattered, or turned on, I thought. But I already knew the answer. Just like his scent had made me soaking wet, mine was making him hard. I watched through my eyelids as his cock engorge. *How does she take that?* I thought, *that would rip me in half.*

"Ace?" Tara's voice called. He jumped away, moving back to the stairs.

"It was nothing," he said, "she's dreaming."

"Let her," she said, "come back to bed."

There was silence for a moment, and then: "What were you doing? When I found you?" She asked.

"What do you mean?" Ace said.

"Her hand was on your chest?" She said.

"She was healing me," he said, "I had a wound. Listen, what's your deal with her? You're acting off."

"I don't know… call it witch's intuition. Somethings not right with her. Don't know what it is. But the evidence all points to something really bad, if One Eye and a vamp are hunting her."

"That's not her fault," Ace said.

"Don't get distracted by a pretty face," Tara said.

"I — I'm not—" Ace blubbered.

"Shh. Don't lie. Just because you love me doesn't mean you'll never be attracted to anyone else. It's okay. I just want you to watch your back. I want both of us to. We can't trust her," she said.

"Yeah, well. We won't need to worry about it when we get her to Castle Rock. Nice going, with the 'school' bit. I don't think she would have agreed if she knew it basically a containment facility for loose cannons."

My heart froze. *Containment facility?* I thought. *They're sending me to fucking jail?*

"She doesn't need to know. She'll be safe there, anyway, until we can figure out what to do with her," Tara said.

Their conversation continued, but I couldn't hear them. *They is no way I'm letting them stick me on some rock now. Oh no. I should have never trusted a cop.*

When their conversation ended and I heard Ace begin to softly snore, I stood, gathering my things. I pulled on the flannel and jeans that Tara had given me, although both were slightly too big. I did this all without making a sound. Then I moved, tiptoeing, to the other side of the room, where Ace had left my dad's leather jacket. He'd had the blood cleaned out, and it smelled fresh. A pretty sweet thing to do, all things considered. I slipped into it, and it fit like a second skin. Then I slipped into the pair of leather boots Tara had given me, and, very carefully, snuck out the door.

The night was cool. I looked up again, at the infinite stars. The island really was a beautiful place. But I never liked staying in one place too long — the last time I had a home, I had a family, too. No place would be the same without them.

I set off through the woods, down the dirt road. The air was cold, but my dad's leather jacket was solidly made, military edition. The wind didn't bite as much. I had a rucksack over one shoulder, filled with essentials: a blanket, spare clothes, some food and water. I was pretty sure I knew the way out of the woods, just from following the drive on the way here. But Ace had mentioned that the woods were dangerous at night, and the island sometimes change; I wanted a back up in case I got lost.

As I walked, I got angrier and angrier. They thought they could lock me up? Put me in some castle like a princess, throw away the key? Well, tough shit. Nobody locks up Anastasia Walker. *That's not true,* I thought, *you just were locked up. For an undisclosed amount of time. With no memories.*

Shit, I thought. Maybe I was overreacting. I knew I did that; I used to see a shrink for PTSD when I was in the system. But that hadn't helped me so much.

I kept walking, but as I did, tears started pouring down my face. My breath grew heavier, more ragged, and suddenly, I needed to stop walking. I leaned against a tree, trying to steady my breath, but the tears kept coming. I wound up sliding down the tree trunk to the forest floor, trying to measure my breath. *It's a panic attack, Ana, you know this. Breathe in for ten seconds, out for ten seconds. In for ten seconds, out for ten seconds.*

But the ten seconds seemed impossibly long, and breath shook and shattered as it left my lungs. Instead, the world around me seemed to disappear, and I was plunged back to the night. *That* night.

It was wicked hot in the house. The AC broke, and it was the peak of summer. I lay on my bed, sweat soaked sheets clinging to my small body. I couldn't sleep, even with all the windows open; the crickets kept me awake. My brother snored softly in the room next to me, and downstairs, my parents were talking. It was a small house, but a happy one. It was the last night I can ever remember being happy.

Suddenly, a gasp. My mother, screaming. Then a crash — fighting.

"Where is she?" A voice said. It was a snobby voice, with a strange accent.

"Not here," my mother said.

My father roared, and I heard a gunshot. Then, the snobby man's laugh and the sound of a body hitting the floor. "Mark!" My mother cried.

"Do not pity the mortal. He is not her true father, you and I both know that. So tell me: where is the girl?"

"Get out of my house! I command it!" My mother said. Again, the hum of magic in the air, the sound of crashing.

"Tsk tsk. You know that your fledgling power is too weak to defeat me. So why try? Do you really love the little abomination so?"

My mother let out a primal scream. I watched as water flowed from everywhere in the house — from my bedside table, from the faucet in the bathroom across the hall — and to where she fought, downstairs.

And then, some of the water came for me. It enveloped me in a cocoon. I struggled against it, but it swallowed me, womblike. I was left floating in a bubble, just above my bed.

From downstairs, flashing lights and huge, thunderous noises. Then, fire. I watched it move up from the kitchen, up the stairs, into my bedroom. It moved in a wall, consuming everything in its path.

The house exploded around me, covered the bubble of water with white-hot flame.

I blacked out as the fire nearly boiled me alive. It was like it was a living thing, trying to eat its way past the protective spell my mother had cast.

I awoke, ash covered, in the ruins of our house. A fireman, lifting me out of the rubble.

The only Walker left alive.

* * *

A sound, in the woods next to me. I heard something like creaking wood. It was enough to snap me out of my trauma flashback, but not enough to calm me down. My throat still wheezed as I breathed. Another sound, this one like breaking branches. Something big was waiting just off the road, right in front of me.

Shaking, I raised a hand to the air. I called on my magic, pulling water from the air. Then I commanded it: *Illuminate.*

The water began to glow softly, then burst into light, illuminating the road in a flash.

Two eyes flashed in the wood; yellow, misshapen eyes. Set in a bare, bald, human-like head. The body of the thing was long and pale, with fleshy, bruised skin. The creature wore tattered clothes, nothing more than rags. It was twice the height of a normal person, but thin, like it was made of elongated bones just barely covered in skin.

It opened its mouth, and I heard that creaking sound, like wood. I realized it was the thing's jaw, making that sound. Like an old door hinge opening. As it extended the mouth, far too wide, I saw rows and rows of rotten, yellowing human teeth.

Oh. Fuck.

The creature flashed towards me. It shambled, long limbs bending at awkward angle. It released a sound something between a hiss, a roar, and a human scream.

I pushed myself backward against the tree, helpless trying to get away. I couldn't. I collapsed back in the dirt, and instead tried to summon a spell. But my terror made it impossible to concentrate.

I managed a weak ice-spear that plunked into the creature's shoulder. Black blood oozed, but the creature still shambled forward. It closed in. I screamed, throwing my hands up to protect my face—

A bright light.

Heat like a roaring blaze.

And the creature, screaming.

I opened my eyes, looked through my fingers. The creature was on fire.

Another jet of flame erupted from my right, spouting like from a flamethrower. Except it was coming from Tara's outstretched hand. "Get behind me!" She shouted.

I scrambled behind her, just as the creature tucked its head and ran. It disappeared, blackened and burned, into the woods.

I panted, trying to catch my breath.

"What... the fuck... was *that!*" I said.

"Wendigo. Old cannibal spirits," she said, "probably wanted to eat your face off. You're lucky I got here when I did."

I chuffed, crossing my arms. "I could have handled it," I said.

"Oh yeah? That's not what it looked like," she said.

I opened my mouth, then closed it.

She laughed. "It's okay. We all have performance anxiety from time to time."

I looked away. If that was what she wanted to think, sure. I didn't want her to know I was having a panic attack. "So, what. Are you going to try and take me back?" I said.

She shrugged. "Personally? I don't care if you live or die, to be honest. But Ace would be upset. He's always collecting strays," she said.

"Okay, so... fine. I'll just be on my way," I said.

"Fine," she said, shrugging.

"Fine!" I said. I started walking away.

"Watch out!" She screamed.

I immediately ducked, raising my hands in a defensive

position. I looked out at the woods, but they were completely silent. From behind me, I heard Tara laughing.

"That was priceless," she said.

"Bitch," I spat.

"Oh come on," she said, following after me, "is it really so bad staying on the island for a little while longer?"

"If everyone is like you? Yeah," I said, "and staying on the island is not the same thing as being a prisoner."

"Ah. I take it you heard Ace and I talking," she said.

"Yeah, not the only thing I heard. By the way, you sound like a horse when you cum," I said.

Her face whitened in a satisfying way.

"Look — Castle Rock is the only place you'll be safe. You really wanna go? Fine. I'll escort you off the island myself. But how far do you really think you're going to make it?"

"I've done fine up until now," I said, "I don't need anyone's help."

"I get it. You're powerful. But One Eye is on a different level. He's been collecting power for centuries; at his peak, his followers were worshipping him as a god. Do you really want to go up against that?"

"I impaled him on an icicle," I said, "some god."

"He's probably still weak from crossing over from Faerie. But that won't last long. There's nowhere left to run, Ana."

I closed my eyes. Deep down, I knew she was right. Where was I going to go? No one could keep me safe. My best bet was trusting these people, and yet I couldn't bring myself to.

"Here, listen. You're powerful, but you've never had much training. Let me help you. That's what Castle Rock is for: helping newer supernaturals control their power. It's not a prison; it's more like a halfway house. Come to Castle Rock, and I'll help train you. Then, when you've learned how to defend yourself — properly defend yourself — you can go."

"Yeah? Just like that" I said.

"Just like that," she said, raising her hands in offering.

I looked at her: beautiful, powerful, collected. Thirty and

already the leader of the whole island. I knew — as much as I already loathed her — that there was a lot I could learn from her.

"Only until we figure this out," I said, "then I'm gone."

"Deal."

I turned, ready to push past her and towards the cabin. She grabbed my arm, whispering in my ear. "And Ana? Stay the fuck away from my boyfriend."

CHAPTER 10

The next morning, Tara made coffee. I was tired and grumpy, and still a little shook up. Ace was grinning ear to ear, whistling and dancing in the kitchen. He was shirtless in an apron, cooking up eggs and sausage. Probably cheery because he spent all night fucking, instead of having your face nearly eaten off by a cannibal monster.

Ace served up hot coffee — black, because he remembered — and hot eggs and sausage. I savored the grease and spice, countered with the bitter richness of the coffee. *God, the food on this island is fucking good.*

The squad car was ruined, so we had to take Tara's truck. It was a vintage baby blue ford, like it came out of an old movie. All metal and rust. Perfect for her. She hopped in the front seat, started the ignition. Ace climbed in next to her.

"What are you waiting for?" Tara said.

"There's no room," I said, "it's only two seats."

"Just hop on his lap," Tara said.

"What?" Ace said.

"What?" I said, even louder.

"Maybe she can just ride in the bed," he said.

"Yeah — I'm not sitting on his lap," I said.

"Bed is full," Tara said. She looked suspiciously between me and Ace. "What's the problem?" She said. *She's testing us. Seeing if we're attracted to one another.*

"Nothing. Nothing, babe," Ace said.

"Come on, Ana, get in," she said.

I scowled, then climbed onto Ace's lap. He froze as if terrified. My hair hung in curtains over his face. When I sat, I could feel his bulge beneath his jeans. I tucked my knees to my chest; I could easily fit entirely on his lap, but I didn't want to be seen laying all over him. Tara looked at us, smiling. *What's your game?* I thought, *just make us uncomfortable? Try to catch us together? Well, guess what, bitch, I don't want your fucking boyfriend.*

Tara pulled out of the dirt driveway. We drove out of the woods, passed the ruined cruiser and the spot where the Wendigo attacked me. Soon, we were driving along the lakeshore. The day was bright blue, a perfect minnesotan spring day. The shore was rocky, and seagulls coasted in the sky, looking for fish. Deer crossed the road in front of us, and I watched them disappear into the woods near a tumbling waterfall.

"It's beautiful here," I said.

"One of the reasons why we keep it to ourselves," Tara said, "the energy here makes it warmer than other places this far north, and things grow better."

"What energy?" I asked. I wanted to talk about anything at all, to keep from thinking about Ace underneath me. He smelled clean today, like fresh deodorant and peppermint soap.

"It's complicated. The island was created as a fortress for a god in the Dawn Age," Tara said.

"You keep saying that," I said.

"What?"

"Dawn Age. What does that mean?" I said.

Tara looked like she wanted to chide me again, for not knowing anything. Instead, Ace stepped in. "It's when Faerie Kings still walked the earth. You ever read Fairy Tales?" He said.

"Yeah — I mean, when I was in middle school, a bit. Like Sleeping Beauty and stuff? Lots of rape," I said.

Tara snorted. "Yeah. That, but real."

"You're telling me Rapunzel built this island?" I said.

"No. The Fae Kings of Old, when they ruled here."

"So whose island is this? Which king's?" I asked.

"No one knows. One of the old Faerie Kings. If he even had a name, it's lost to time," she said, shrugging. "What we do know for sure is that Ogen One Eye took it over, when he first came to North America. Then this island was his for centuries. He ran the supernatural world from Castle Rock."

I stopped. "The place you're taking me right now — this impregnable fortress — is his old house?"

"More or less, yeah," she said.

"What the hell! What if he kept a spare key?" I said.

"It doesn't work like that," Tara said.

Ace spoke up. "You know, she's got a point," he said.

"No, she doesn't," Tara said, shooting him a glare. "The fortress is bound to us now. The people of Myston. It won't betray us."

I leaned back on the window. "Great. I'm fucked," I said.

I shifted on Ace's lap.

That's when I felt it. Something… hard.

Oh my god, I thought, *does he have a boner right now?*

I stole a look down at him. He was breathing quickly, trying to control himself, but color rose in his cheeks. His eyes flashed golden, and he turned away, looking for any excuse.

Don't move an inch, I thought, *you'll only make it worse.*

But I felt a tickle between my legs. The feel of his hard cock was making me wet. *Fuck. Fuck, fuck, fuck!*

The tension between us was palpable. *Tara can't see.*

"There it is!" Ace shouted.

Thank God.

The fortress was a huge block of stone just off the coast, on a rocky island next to the larger one. A lone road led to it, on a bulwark made of stones. Tara took a right onto the road, and we pulled up before the fortress. It looked old and new at the same time: it was all stone, but the stone wasn't worn at all. It could have been built for the revolutionary war, or even yesterday.

There was a single portcullis that was down. In the center, a lighthouse tower rose into the sky, its flame burning.

Castle Rock.

The portcullis opened and we drove through, into an open air courtyard. Tara parked the car, and I instantly threw the door open, hopping off of Ace's hard dick. He instantly covered himself.

Tara stepped out, but Ace stayed inside.

"You coming, babe?" She asked.

"I'm good for right now," he said, smiling awkwardly.

She shrugged. "Suit yourself."

A voice came from the central tower of Castle Rock, at the large wooden entryway. "Oh look, it's the girl who tried to kill me."

I turned to see Grayson, the cat shifter who'd patched me up, standing in the doorway.

Tara stepped forward and gave Grayson a hug. "I haven't heard that story," she said.

"Yeah, and then she made your boyfriend strip to his underwear," he said.

My face flushed.

"Did she, now?" Tara said, "Fascinating."

I put my hand behind my head, looking at the floor. "Yeah — sorry about that. You were helping. I was scared."

Grayson nodded. "Apology accepted. I gotta admit, I was pretty impressed. Not everyone can get a jump on Ace."

Ace — who apparently had settled his erection down well enough to stand — walked around the car and shook Grayson's hand. "She didn't get the jump on me. I was just playing along."

"Sure you were," I said, "tighty-whities."

He rolled his eyes. "Get a new joke, kid," he said.

Tara leaned over and gave him a smooch. "Aw, I like his tighty-whities."

Yeah, I heard — all last night, I thought.

When she kissed Ace, I saw something in Grayson's eyes. *Jealousy? Interesting.*

"Come on. I'll show you your room," Grayson said. I followed him inside. The main chamber of Castle Rock was the lighthouse, and it opened into a bright tower. Mezzanines circled the interior.

"Whoah," I said, looking up.

"Yeah, I know. Pretty insane. Literally living in a Faerie King's castle," he said.

"And this is where you keep your delinquent witches?" I said.

"More than that," he said, "it's where we run the whole island. Everyone knows if there's ever an attack, go to Castle Rock. It's supposed to be impregnable. Think of it like a school, a town hall, and a barracks all in one."

"Multipurpose. How economical," I said.

He smiled. "Come on. I'll show you the bunks," he said.

He took me up some stairs, around the mezzanine, and to a large chamber. The windows looked out over the lake, and the walls were lined with bunk beds. "Hey y'all," Greg said, "newbie incoming."

A muscular kid jumped up from his cot and looked at me: he had big brown eyes and close cropped black hair, and looked to be of Latinx descent. He looked at me wide-eyed, stood, and then shook my hand. "Al," he said, "nice to meet you."

A girl with dark skin and braids sauntered over from the windows. "What's her deal?" She said.

"Why does everyone in this town pretend like I'm not here?" I said. I appraised the girl; she wore a white blouse and jeans.

"Selena, this is Anastasia Walker. She'll be staying here for a while," Grayson said.

"Okay but why," she said, "what's her deal?"

"I'm being hunted by a Wolf God and an immortal bounty hunter," I said, "one of which apparently returned from the dead just to lock me up and do god knows what to me, and then take my memories."

Selena stared, mouth open. "Uhhh…."

"And I hoped we learned a valuable lesson about asking personal questions," I said. I moved to the side of the room and threw my shit on a bunk. *Out of the asshole frying pan, into the asshole fire,* I thought.

I lay down on the cot and closed my eyes.

At least, here, I might be safe.

But the sound of the man that killed my parents rang in my ears. *Where is she?*

And I knew.

I would never be safe.

CHAPTER 11

I decided it was time for a hot shower. That had always been my escape from the world, and I felt like I needed that right about now. I took the soap and towel that Ace had left me and headed to the dorm bathroom, an ancient stone room retrofitted with showers and toilets. It reminded me of some the group homes I lived in as a kid; tacky, cheap decor that was worn down by thousands of hands over time. Some Fairy Castle, I thought, and then, wait... do Faeries even need to use the shower? Or toilet? When was this all added in?

I shook the thought away. The last thing I wanted to think about was the supernatural world. Being a witch had only ever been my way to make money; it wasn't a religion, or even a lifestyle. It was food on the table and a switchblade in my pocket. That was it.

I turned on the shower and found it was blissfully hot. I let the water wash the sweat and dirt and grime from my body; I hadn't bathed since I'd washed up on the shore of the island, and I wouldn't consider Lake Superior a bath. I considered a long hot shower to be a form of meditation; I let my mind wander, or go blank. I crafted the water with magic, made designs and glowing orbs and spirals of liquid. I wondered if I could water scry like Tara had done with her flame. Maybe, if I played along, she would teach me.

I started thinking of Ace. Of his body, his soft cock when

he checked on me. The hot water poured over me, and I couldn't help myself. I reached down to play with my pussy. It was so wet and warm, even in the hot shower. I ground my vulva against my hand, gently gasping as I slipped one finger inside and then slipped it out, using the wetness to play with my clit. I started slow, working up the feeling there, until it felt like an electric current of pleasure each time I moved my finger. I put my other fingers in my mouth, to keep from moaning, but also imagining it was Ace's cock, stretching me out. I wanted him to use my throat like I was his bad little girl, like I was his plaything. Then he would flip me over and lick my pussy, taste it, so that I could feel his rough tongue and scratchy beard. Then, when he'd had his fill of my scent, he'd press the tip of his huge cock against my clit. He'd rub it around, teasing me, until I begged for him to slide it in.

He'd oblige. Just an inch at first. Then, when I screamed that I wanted him to fuck me, please, all the way, he'd slide the length of his girth into me. That huge, wet cock, pounding against my tight hole. *Please*, I'd say. *Please*. Maybe he'd get out the faerune cuffs and lock them behind my back, so I couldn't fight back. Maybe he'd call me his good girl when I took all of him inside me.

I pictured him mounting me, shifting between his hybrid form and his human form, his claw-like hands wrapped around my throat. His hairy adonis belt grinding into me, watching as his huge cock ruined me forever. He would be my god; my master. And after he was done taking me for his own, he would shove that wet cock right in my mouth, make me taste and lick my own perfume. Then, gripping my cheeks, he would release his huge load on my face.

And I'd beg for more.

I came.

I came hard, letting a moan as I clamped down over my mouth.

I stood shaking in the shower, totally spent. The room spun. Did I feel bad for touching myself to Ace? Sure. Was it preferable to keeping the attraction bottled up? Hell yes.

I rinsed off and stepped out of the shower only to see someone standing outside. I jumped, nearly slipping on the tile floor. I prepared to reach for my magic, fend off another threat.

Then, the person came into focus: dark brown skin, braids, wrapped in a white towel. Selena.

"Jesus Christ!" I shouted, "I was about to hex you."

She arched an eyebrow. "You mean, you were about to try to hex me. You'd never land a hit."

Maybe it was because I was still shocked, but my magic reached out and grabbed all the water in the room. The steam in the air turned to icy mist, and the water on the floor slicked into a sheet of deadly ice. The temperature in the room dropped fifty degrees, and Selena looked at her breath, steaming the air.

"Whoah, whoah," she said, "claws away. I didn't mean to scare you, I just wanted to shower."

I exhaled, releasing my hold on the water. Ice melted and snowflakes dropped to the floor like rain. "Sorry," I said, "force of habit."

Selena laughed awkwardly. "Well, damn. That was some trick. You've got power on you, I can feel it."

"You're a witch?" I asked.

"Mmm-hmm. Earth witch. Didn't know it until I was nineteen, though. Nearly put my grandma's house in a sinkhole. That's when I decided to come here," she said.

"You chose to come here?" I asked, "did you know they were going to stick you on some rock?"

"Yeah — but I figured it was a better alternative than accidentally causing an earthquake or something."

"You can't control your powers?"

She raised an eyebrow. "Not all of us come from magical families," she said, "But I'd wager I know a fair bit more than you, now. I've been hitting the books. I heard about you. Witch mom, right?"

"Dead witch mom," I said, "murdered witch mom. But yeah."

Selena let out a long sigh. "I just keep putting my foot in my mouth, don't I?" She said.

"And I keep being a bitch in return. I'm sorry," I said.

"No, I should be sorry. Look, can we start over? I'm Selena," she said. She extended a hand.

I shook it. "Anastasia. Nice to meet you. Look, anything I should know about this place?"

Selena shrugged. "Keep your head down. Be a good girl. Then that bitch Tara will let you out — if you prove you're not a danger to society."

"She's not so bad," I said, "she saved my life."

Selena smirked. "Just wait. You haven't started training with her yet."

I frowned. I wondered what that would be like.

"So what you guys, some kind of a coven?" I said.

Selena laughed. "Hardly. There's a few more witches in town, but they keep to themselves. And Tara doesn't need anyone but herself. Real firebrand, har-har."

Selena dropped her towel and stood, naked, in front of the shower. I averted my eyes. She stepped into the shower and turned it on, making the room fill with steam.

"Look, I'm sorry we got off on the wrong foot — friends?" She said. She stuck her head from behind the shower curtain.

I nodded hesitantly. "Sure," I said, "friends." I wasn't usually one to make that commitment — I liked being alone. But it didn't seem like I had other options.

She smiled. "Good. But you better not snore."

With that, she tucked into the shower and was gone.

I made my way out of the bathroom and down the hall of the lighthouse. The interior of the tower was spacious, lit with moonlight. I reached out to the water that covered my skin and warmed it, so that it steamed off me in waves.

"Settling in?" A voice said. I turned to see Ace, standing against the wall, his arms folded across his chest. I was acutely aware that I was still in my towel, which only barely covered my body. I gripped it tighter.

"Doing alright," I said.

"Look, I know it's not ideal—"

"Prison on a rock? No, it's basically a Cabo all-inclusive," I said, voice dripping with sarcasm.

"It'll keep you safe," he said. He stepped out of the shadows, and I saw the moonlight slip across his face. My breath caught. His jaw was like a blade. He was the most handsome man I'd ever seen, I realized, and my body called out to him. *There's something special here,* I thought, *something powerful.*

He stepped towards me, put a hand on my arm. Again, I could smell his musk, his cologne. "I will protect you," he said.

I looked up at him. In the moonlight, his face seemed almost blue, like it was underwater.

For a moment we just stood there, breathing.

"What are you doing?" I asked.

He stared at me, blue eyes wide. Then he dropped his hand and took a step back.

"Sorry," he said, "I shouldn't have—"

I thought about what Tara had said. *Stay the fuck away from my boyfriend.*

"Yeah," I said, "you shouldn't have."

And I turned and walked away, letting him watch me go.

CHAPTER 12

I stood in the spacious gymnasium that was used for lessons. People mingled about with their instructors. Ace mentored the shifters, speaking confidently to the five or six assembled. Many were young; as I understood it, most shifters were born with the power. Very few came to weild it through transformation or infection. He was sexy when he controlled them; I could see the alpha inside that Tara seemed to suppress. Maybe she's using magic on him? Could explain a bit.

Selena watched Ace with heavily lidded eyes; I could see her admiring him from afar. When Ace went behind a female shifter to fix her fighting stance, the girl shivered under his touch.

Tara entered the gym, then called over the witches. There were three of us: Selena, myself, and a wispy girl of Asian descent named Mae. She didn't seem all to interested in talking to us, but I gleaned from Selena that she was a 'moon witch.' That was a pretty rare alignment, as far as I knew. Most witches were bonded to one of the four physical elements: air, water, fire, or earth. But theoretically, a witch could aligned to almost anything. Light, spirit, shadow, life, crystals. The alignment didn't limit the spells a witch could perform, but it did make certain spells easier. Water called out to me, and I could control it. Fire, not so much.

There were a few other groups of students at the school —

besides witches and shifters, there were various fairbloods, AKA people with fae ancestry. Half elves, half orcs, goblins, etc. It was the first time I'd ever met someone who had real Fae ancestry; I'd thought they were just a myth. But those types tended to keep to themselves, and I rarely saw them. They weren't in the gym today. There were two half-vampires that kept to themselves, practicing sparring. I looked at their pale skin and red eyes and was reminded of the vampire bounty hunter that had attacked us in the woods.

Tara led us to a corner of the room, inside a circle of painted runes.

"What is this?" I asked.

Tara frowned, folding her arms. "I call it the Playground. Spells can't enter or leave. And damage from spells is dampened; less likely one of you gets killed," she said.

She reached into a duffle bag and brought out a rumpled book. She handed it to me.

"A spell book?" I asked. I'd never had one before; the only one I'd ever seen had been my mother's and that had burned in the fire. "It's printed. I would have thought it was written in blood, or something."

"Consider it training wheels. You only cast out of that book. Understand?" Tara said.

I flipped through the pages: the spells were a mixture of incantations and pre-set runes. "I've only ever cast intuitively before."

"Not in Myston. Here, you follow the rules," she said, "cast from the book, or not at all."

"But that's—"

"No argument," she snapped. "Now, watch Selena and Mae spar. No elements."

"No elements! Are you kidding!" I said, "that's all I know how to do!"

"And that's why you're a danger to the town, Ana. Elements are controlled with emotions, not logic — you need to learn to bare bones of magic, if you want any real kind of control."

I clenched my teeth. *I'll show you control,* I thought. But I stepped outside of the Playground and let Selena and Mae take the stage. They each had their own spell books, hastily printed and worn. They held them in their open palms, hands dangling above the page.

I sat on the bleachers as they began to spar. Their books began to glow, and runes floated out of them. They could cast the prewritten spells with a flick of their hand or a spoken word of the Faetounge.

Their spells flickered, creating effects: bursts of sparks or gusts of wind, icy spears or shields of light. Their words echoed off the walls of the gym. I flipped through the spell book, trying to locate worthwhile battle spells. *Bullshit. I could do more than these if she gave me some water.*

I looked over to where Ace stood with his shifters. He'd shifted to hybrid form, with a man's body covered in hair and a wolf's head. Then he shifted in a flash to full wolf form, huge and snarling. He explained something to his students, and they shifted between their forms: a weretiger got stuck between forms, twitching on the ground.

Ace helped him back to human form, and patted him on the back. They were both naked; shifters tended to learn pretty quickly that nudity didn't matter. They were part animal, after all. I tried not to look at the way his muscled curved as he helped the other shifter up. *Fuck, he's kind, too. A kind alpha — who would have thought?* Or at least he was caring. Fatherly.

In the Playground, Selena had constructed some kind of light prison around Mae. Mae sent her spells futilely against it.

"Enough!" Tara said, "match goes to Selena."

Selena smirked, releasing her spell over Mae. Mae scowled, then marched out of the Playground.

"Ana, you're up," Tara said.

Fuck. Should have studied instead of ogling Hot Cop.

I stood on the bleachers, clutching the spell book to my chest. I stepped forward, into the Playground, and faced up to

Selena.

She smirked. "Ready to get those claws out?" She said.

I frowned. After what she did to Mae, and without my water magic, I wasn't confident I could beat her. "I—"

"She's not dueling you, Selena," Tara said, stepping in the ring. "She's dueling me."

Selena and Mae shared a glance. "But Tara…" Mae started.

"You'll fuck her up!" Selena finished.

Tara eyed me, arcing around the circle like a stalking cat. "I'm not so sure. If Ace is to be believed, this one threw a vampire miles out to sea."

Selena and Mae both looked at me; Selena arched an eyebrow and cocked her head, sticking a hip out to one side. "Huh. She failed to mention that."

I ignored them. Instead, I faced Tara. "You sure about this?" I said.

I looked over her shoulder. To my surprise — and dismay — I saw that Ace and the other shifters had stopped to watch.

"Better me than Selena or Mae," Tara said, "and besides. I've been curious."

"Have it your way," I said, and raised my spell book.

She smirked, raising her own.

"To capture or submission," she said. "Selena, count us down."

Selena frowned, looking worried. "One… two… thre—"

Before she could even say 'three,' Tara had whipped a spell from the pages of her book. A searing whip of white hot light lashed out and struck me, throwing me against the back wall of the ring. The shields stopped me from flying out, but I still landed painfully on the floor. My spell book flew from my hand, sliding away from me.

"What's the matter, Soppy?" Tara said.

I pushed up onto one arm, grimacing. "Soppy? Seriously?" I said.

"Because you're a water witch," she said, "figured it was a good nick name. Cute."

I rolled my eyes. "Your attempt at witty banter makes me want to attempt suicide," she said.

Tara frowned. "That's sad, Soppy," she said, "now get up."

I breathed heavily. "Actually, I'm fine down here. Why don't you join me?"

I stuck my hand out and sent a gravity spell hurtling at Tara. It struck her in the chest, and she felt backwards, stuck to the floor.

"Hah! Soppy that, bitch," I said.

Tara shouted a counter curse and dispelled the magic trapping her. Then, in a moment, we were on our feet. "So you're not completely useless without water magic," she said, "good to know."

I shrugged. "You learn to be resourceful, living on the streets."

Tara lifted a spell from the book in her hand; it curled around her fingers, rings of golden glowing runes. She sent it at me, and I deflected it: it struck the forcefield around the edge of the ring, exploding in a shatter of golden light. I lifted a spell from my own book, and sent it flying at her. She deflected and returned the curse, and it struck me in the shoulder, sending a patina of ice over my leather jacket. I hissed in pain and clutched the icicle forming there.

"That might be so," she said, "but nothing replaces a good education. I trained at Hollowbridge Academy. With the best supernaturals in the world."

I grimaced, using a heating spell to melt the ice from my shoulder. "So high and mighty," I said, "why don't we take off the training wheels? I'll use my element, you use yours. Then we see who really comes out on top."

She frowned. A spell hovered at her fingertips, green wisps swirling in the air. "You'd like that, wouldn't you," she sneered.

"What, are you afraid?" I said, "scared of what the little street witch will do to all your big, expensive education?"

Ace and the other shifters had stopped sparring and were watching intently. His eyes burned with — what? Worry?

Fascination? Even the two half vampires had stopped to stare.

Tara looked over her shoulder at Ace. *She wants to impress him,* I realized, *she likes being on top.* Witches didn't have Alphas, but if they did, Tara would be the Alpha in Myston. *Maybe not for long.*

"Come on, Sparky. Let's see what you've got."

Tara's face twisted into a snarl. Her hand exploded in flame, and she thrust it towards me, dropping the spell book. I smiled. If elements were on the field, I was a whole different witch.

The fireball flashed in front of me. I reached into the air, pulling water from it. It coalesced in front of me, forming a shield just as the fireball crashed into it. The water shield erupted into steam, and I felt the flames lick my skin, frighteningly near. *Too close. I need more water.*

I reached out into the air, but my spell died at the edge of the ring. *The ward spells won't let me take water from outside of the ring. This is all I've got.*

The blob of water floated in the air near me, only the size of a baseball. *It's not enough,* I thought, just as another fireball ripped towards me. The shield held stronger this time, only because I solidified it into ice. Still, Tara's fire evaporated it in an instant, and I had to gather it from the air again.

Time to go on the offensive. Go! Now!

I sent my precious water at her in the form of an ice spear. She created a shield of fire, and the ice spear evaporated. But for a moment she was knocked off balance. I ripped the water back towards me, then sent it at her again in a blizzard. It struck her in the face, and she staggered, flames still roaring from her hands. She sent them out in arcs, wildly, without control.

One of the flame whips flashed, too close. I felt a burst of flame in my leg, searing and hot, like I'd been stabbed. I looked down; my jeans had burned away, leaving only charred, black flesh beneath.

I growled. Something came over me, ancient and powerful. It said, *you are hurt, you are in danger.* And my magic reached out, without my permission, into the air. It hit the edge of the ring, where the dampening spell was. And then it pushed outwards, crumbling the spell into dust. I heard screams around the room, but barely registered them. I could see blue wisps of power rising from my skin.

My magic spread further, deeper. It found water in the walls, in pipes, under the ground. I raised a hand and ripped them all up. The gymnasium floor exploded, bringing water to the surface. It rushed out of the broken floor like a geyser.

Then it crushed Tara. I saw her fly backwards, like she was caught in an unending riptide.

She burst out of the crumbling shields around us, slammed into the back wall of the gymnasium.

Chaos surrounded me. Blue light filled my vision, then vanished, followed by blackness.

I stood, alone, empty, in the wreckage.

Then I fell, completely drained of magic.

Before I closed my eyes, I saw Ace's hulking form over me, kneeling. His face was filled with fear.

CHAPTER 13

"What the fuck was that," Selena said. She stood over my bed, talking with Ace. My eyes were still closed, and I pretended to be unconscious.

"No clue. Tara might have a better idea, once she wakes up. But it seems our mystery witch has a secret,"Ace said.

Selena scoffed. "You're telling me. I've never met a witch that wielded that amount of elemental power. She ripped up groundwater. Through, like, layers of stone. What the hell? Who is she?"

"That's what I've been trying to figure out," Ace said, "I knew something was off the minute she washed up on the island. It's like, when she's threatened, her magic takes over. It won't let her get hurt."

"Yeah, and it nearly killed your girlfriend," Selena said.

"She'll be fine. She's tough, and Grayson is working on her right now. In the meantime, we need to figure out what to do with Ana."

"Can't we kick her out? Just cut our losses, tell her to leave?" Selena said. My heart dropped. Of course, that would make the most sense. It did for anyone else who tried to take me in.

"Selena—" Ace started.

"What? I'm being realistic. She's dangerous, Ace. To you, to me, probably to the whole town," she said, "Look, I like her, personally, I really do — but no one is worth letting the whole island get hit by a tsunami. We keep her around, and Myston might become the next Atlantis."

"We can't. Not when everyone else has thrown her out on her ass. That's what Myston does — we protect people. We care for each other. She saved me from the vampire. That means I owe her, and if I owe her, the pack owes her. She stays. End of discussion."

I could almost hear Selena frowning, even with her eyes closed. "Well. I guess she's better on our side than on Ogen's."

"Let's hope," Ace said quietly. "I'm going to check on Tara. You keep the wards up. I'll keep the new shifters on guard."

"Aye, aye, captain!" Selena said.

"And watch the tone," he said. Then Ace's steps faded away, and I faded back into sleep.

* * *

I dreamed. At first it was only of water: of floating in the grey deepness of Lake Superior, blue light swirling around me. My power reached out the far horizons, limitless. Then I was running through a dark wood again, with the white wolf following me. I was naked, and my bare feet bled on the rocky shore. All around me, trees burst into flame, turning the blue night into a sickly blood red.

I tripped, and Ogen pounced on me. I looked into his one eye, only to see that it was a green jewel, glimmering with chaotic power. He snarled, reached out with his open mouth, and —

A flash. A winter's wind. Ogen dissolved into a spray of ash and ice, his howl piercing the night air. I panted, frozen with fear, and pushed myself up on the stone shore.

From my right, the cold wind blew. I saw him rise out of the water, his pale face a perfect mask. His black eyes fixed on me. Around him, all the power and deadliness of winter roared. And atop his head, a crown of ice.

He extended a death-white hand to me. *My beloved,* he said, *come to me.*

* * *

I woke with a start. Cold sweat clung to my face, and my sheets were in a tangle, damp with moisture. *Nightmare, I thought, just a nightmare.* I looked around the room. They'd moved me to a separate chamber near to the top of the lighthouse. It was small, with white stucco walls and nothing but a cot and a small vanity. The window was open to the night air, and white curtains blew inside, billowing in the misty breeze. Moonlight splayed across the floor, illuminating a bare patch of stone.

I stood, moved to the edge of the room where a pitcher of water waited. I wore a white nightgown, and bandages covered the area where Tara had burned me. *Grayson must have patched me up again,* I thought. Then I thought back to the incident in the gym. Why had Ace rushed over to me, and not Tara? Wouldn't he want to make sure his girlfriend was okay?

I poured myself a glass of water and drank deeply; it seemed to refresh me to my very core, and I gasped as cold water dribbled down my chin.

"Thirsty girl," a voice said from behind me.

I whipped around. In the shadows by the window, a tall, pale shape stood. He stepped forward into the moonlight, all pale skin, black leather, and red eyes.

"You," I said, looking at the vampire. I summoned my magic to my hands, and a soft glow appeared, but not much. I'd used everything I had in the fight against Tara.

The vampire raised his hands. "Me," he said, "back for more."

"Stay away from me," I said, "or I'll boil all the blood in your body."

He shrugged. "Even if you had the magic left to do that, you'd have to get past my very powerful and very expensive warding spells." He lifted his arm and pulled down his sleeve; beneath it, I could see extensive tattoos tracing his skin. *Ward magic, bonded to flesh. My spells can hit him, but I can't effect him directly. He's too imbued with magic.*

Still, I let blizzard-wind form in my hands, ready to launch it at him. *It won't kill him, but maybe I can distract him enough to get help.*

"Right now, you're probably thinking — maybe I can distract him long enough to get help, right? The answer to that would be, maybe. But then you won't hear what I have to say."

I looked at him. Like all vampires, he was stunningly beautiful. Pale skin, lithe figure, jaw that could cut glass. He smirked.

"And what is that?" I said.

"That I'm not here to kill you. Or even abduct you," he said.

"If not that, then what?" I said, "has Ogen given up so easily?"

He looked at me, confused, then laughed. His laugh was actually charming, deep and masculine. "You think I work for Ogen? Oh Gods, no. I wouldn't be caught dead working with the mongrels. You do know that vampires and werewolves tend to not get along, right?"

"You're interested in money, not honor," I said, "I figured you didn't care."

"Like I said, girl, not all treasure is silver," he said, "But yes, I seek greater fortune. But no, I do not work for Ogen. Ogen wants you dead. I come with a different option."

I frowned. "What do you mean? Who sent you?"

"Why, your future betrothed. Your fated mate. The one whose blood sings out to yours, who calls you to be his queen," he said, smiling.

"I don't know what you're talking about," I said. The room suddenly felt cold. The magic I was preparing died in my hand, the cold light flickering out.

"You don't? You don't feel him, on the other side of the Veil? Waiting?" He said. "He never comes to you in dreams?"

I froze. I thought of the nightmare I'd had just before the vampire arrived. About a frozen king coming to offer me his hand, defeating Ogen. *Could it be a coincidence?*

The vampire smiled again, then bowed deeply, flaring

his hand behind his back. "Perhaps proper introductions are in order. I am Varnei, the vampire. And I come as an envoy from Farien, Winter's King, Lord of the Winter Court of Faeries, master of the Dark Sidhe."

Fae. Like Tara and Ace had said. Unbelievable strong supernaturals, beings from another world. *This can't be happening. It's a trick.*

"Why should I believe you?" I said. "First you try to kidnap me, and now you claim I'm some of Faerie King's lost girlfriend?"

"I regret my actions earlier," Varnei said, "I only wish I had been more respectful of you. My lord was simply impatient for his mate, and I wanted oh so much to please him."

Again, his knowing smirk. "But if it makes you feel better, he has sent a gift. Here:"

Varnei produced a blue velvet box from his coat. He tossed it to me, and I caught it one hand.

"Open it," he said.

Cautiously, I opened the box. Inside was a a simple charm bracelet of polished silver. In the moonlight, it gleamed like it was made of ice. Around the bracelet, charms shaped like snowflakes hung, each made what seemed to be diamond. It was cold to the touch, but not painfully so — it left a painful tingle on her skin.

"Inside that bracelet is a signal; if you are in danger, rub the snowflake until it melts, and Lord Farien will send aid."

I stared at the enchanted bracelet once more.

"What does he want from me in return?" I asked, closing the lid.

Varnei smiled. "Nothing but your love," he said, "and undying devotion. He wishes for you to wait for his arrival. When he does arrive, he shall claim you as his queen."

I frowned. "I'm not a trophy," I said.

"He knows. You are so much more," he said, "but I warn you, Anastasia. My lord is a jealous man, and not forgiving. If your eye wanders, he might not look kindly on whoever it lands on. Tread lightly."

"Well you can tell King Whatshisface that I don't even know him, and my eye will wander wherever it god damn—"

A whisper of curtains. I turned to see that the place Varnei had occupied was gone, and I stood alone in the room.

"—please." I finished.

The room seemed to echo with that final word. I waited for any sound to indicate that he was still outside, watching, but the window remained empty except for the bright eye of the moon.

Creep, I thought.

I was too rattled to go back to bed, so I decided I'd better tell Ace and Tara about the visit from Varnei. I didn't know if they'd want to see me, especially Tara, but I figured they'd at least want to know that a powerful vampire had somehow slipped through their wards.

When I went to the door, I found it was locked.

Deadbolted.

Those assholes, I thought, *they locked me in!*

I sighed, then laid back down in bed. It was all too much. A Wolf God trying to kill me. A Faerie King trying to bed me. Why? What was so special about me?

Unable to answer, I turned over in bed and slept.

CHAPTER 14

"Y**ou** saw what?" Tara said, eyes wide. Ace next to her, in my bedroom. It was morning, and each of us held a cup of steaming coffee.

"The vampire. Bounty hunter, whatever. His name is Varnei. He came in the through the window."

Tara stared at her, sputtering. "I-impossible. I set the wards myself, and the Faerie magic should have—"

"Yeah, well, it didn't. Go figure," I said.

Tara tugged at her hair, making red stands bunch in her fingers. She bit her lip, frustrated. *That looks familiar,* I thought.

Ace stepped in. "How are you still here? How did you get away?"

I shrugged. "He said his tactic changed. He was trying to convince me to go with him."

Ace snorted. "What? Why? As if that would work," he said, "wait, what did he say?"

I looked between Tara and Ace. *Can I trust them? Should I keep this to myself?*

"He told me… he said that his boss thinks I'm his fated mate," I said.

"Fated mate," Ace breathed, "like…"

"Like a shifter would have, yeah," I said.

"So he's a shifter? The guy who hired Varnei?" Ace said. "Could be another pack leader."

Tara frowned. "That's unusual, to say the least. Shifters and vamps don't tend to get along," she said.

"He wasn't a shifter," I said, swallowing.

Tara looked at me expectantly. "Well? Who was he?"

"He's, um. Well. He said he was hired by a… king. A Faerie King."

Silence.

Tara and Ace stood perfectly still. Then Ace started to laugh. He hooted, wiping a tear from his eye. "Phew. I thought you were being serious. That's pretty good, I almost shit my pants. Now seriously, who sent him?"

I stared, shrugging my shoulders. My mouth dropped open. *How can I put this?*

Tara ducked her head down. "Ace," she said, "I don't think she's kidding."

She looked beaten down — there were still bruises on her face from where I'd hit her with the water cannon. To her credit, she soldiered on, not really seeming to hold it against me. Instead, she just regarded me as a curiosity. A threat, of course, but an interesting one.

Ace looked to me, then to to Tara. His smile dropped.

"How is that… what are you…. Ana, help us out here!"

"He said it was a Faerie King! I don't know what else to tell you," I said.

Tara sat, placing her head in her hands. Then she looked up, sighing. "The Faerie Kings have been gone from Earth for centuries. Millenia. They haven't been here since the Dawn Age."

"And?" I said.

"If one is searching for you, that's a big deal. A monumental deal. At least it explains how Varnei slipped through Castle Rock's wards. It's faerie magic. His boss must have given him a key."

"You can't be serious, babe," Ace said. He folded his arms, muscles tensing. "This is like saying Napoleon is coming to make you his girlfriend! Like saying Zeus just matched with you on tinder! It's insane!"

"Faeries used to interfere with mortal affairs all the time. If she really is his fated mate, then he's probably been waiting for centuries for her. Did he say which King?"

"Farien," I said, the name strange on my tongue, "Winter's King."

Ace hissed. Tara's head snapped up.

"Are you sure, Ana? Are you sure he said Farien?" Tara said. Ace began pacing.

"Yeah, I mean I'm pretty sure. Hard name to forget. What's the big deal?" I said.

Ace and Tara shared a worried look.

"In the Fairy Stories… Farien was the cruelest and most powerful of the Faerie Kings. He ruled over winter, and with it, death. When he came to lay claim to Earth, it caused the Dark Ages. The Black Plague. Mass slaughter. Harsh winters, famine, wolves."

My skin seemed to freeze. "What does he want with me? I'm just some girl…"

"You're a powerful witch. Maybe the most powerful I've ever seen, if yesterday's showing is any indication," Tara said, "and Faeries are all about power. And if you really are his fated mate, he won't stop until he has you."

I shivered, thinking of the creature in my dreams. Pure black eyes. Bone pale skin. A crown of ice, and all of Winter at his fingertips.

I looked to Ace. He'd stopped pacing, and I felt something radiating off of him. Anger? Hatred? Jealousy? I could see, in his eyes, a glimmer of wolfish gold. *His wolf is trying to escape — why?*

"What next?" I asked, "I can't stay here, not when Varnei can come visit whenever he wants. And will you be safe, if Farien comes for me?"

"If Farien comes for you, no one will be safe," she said, "but Fae Kings haven't crossed over into our world since the Dawn Age. To do so would be to violate the Court of Courts."

"Which means…" I said.

"War," Ace growled. His eyes flashed gold.

"War? Between who?" I asked.

"Everyone. Faeries versus shifters. Faeries versus mortals. Vampires, fairbloods, dragons — anyone on Earth who wants Earth to stay alive."

I swallowed. My left hand trembled, and I placed it on the wall to steady myself. "This doesn't make any sense," I said, "I'm no one. I'm a drifter. That's it, I don't want any of this, I don't..."

"It doesn't matter what you want," Tara said, "you came here anyway, and because of that, everyone I love is in danger!"

She stood, and I could feel the rage and fear radiating off of her. "You are a curse," she said, "and I want you gone."

Tara marched to the door. She turned around to look at Ace. "Are you coming?" She asked.

Ace looked between her and me. His mouth dropped open.

"Whatever," Tara sneered. And she vanished out the door.

We stood there for a moment in total silence.

Then I stood, started packing what little I had.

"What are you doing?" Ace said.

"Leaving," I said, "I should have known. I don't belong here."

I shoved the last of my borrowed clothes into the backpack and grabbed my dad's leather jacket. I walked towards the door.

Ace stepped into my way, raising his hands.

"Hey, hey — don't do anything rash, okay? We can figure this out," he said.

I raised an eyebrow. "Oh yeah? We're going to figure out what to do about the King of Winter coming to plunge the world into war, just so he can fuck me? You have a solution?"

He smiled sheepishly, "Well, not exactly..."

"That's what I thought. So move," I said.

I stepped around him; he stepped in front of me again, placing his big hands on my shoulders. Again, that electricity pulsed between us. I could smell him again, the raw man of him, and see into the depths of his blue eyes. His wolf eyes flashed briefly — hungry, horny, desperate.

"Don't," he commanded.

I fought against his grip. He held me still.

"Let me go!" I said.

"No," he growled, "not if you insist on leaving and getting yourself into an even bigger mess! Ogen One Eye is still out there, hunting you!"

"He can have me," I said, "if it means saving the world. I'd rather die."

He looked at me, eyes suddenly deeply sad. "Don't say that," he said, softly.

"Why? Why not? What *am* I to you, Ace? I'm not your girlfriend. I'm not your daughter. I'm not even your friend. I'm a drifter who washed up on your beach. So why don't you stop pretending to care, and get out of my way?"

His eyes looked hurt. He looked as if he were about to say something, but stopped himself. I watched his lips, watched the stubble on his strong jaw, the muscles moving under his white t-shirt. *God, he's so fucking beautiful.*

"Ahem?" A voice came.

Ace turned around. Selena stood in the doorway, arms folded. "I think she said let her go. Or do I have to remind you what the word *no* means, Wolfboy?"

A flicker of green magic twisted around her left hand.

Ace dropped my arm. He looked back and forth, fuming. Then he marched out the door.

Selena watched him go. The she turned back to me, a curious expression on her face.

"You good?" She said.

"Yeah," I said, "yeah. We were just talking."

"Pretty passionate conversation," she said, stepping in to the room. She closed the door behind her with a flick of her hand.

"What's that supposed to mean?" I said.

Selena plopped down on the bed. "Oh, nothing. Just that I see him watching you."

"So?" I scoffed, "I'm threat level midnight apparently, so I'd watch me too."

"Not like that," she said, "and I'm good with emotions. Call me an empath, if you want. And I see something, moving between you too. Something strong."

I froze. *That feeling,* I thought, *can she see it?*

I started to speak, but she cut me off. "Don't bother lying," she said.

I groaned, then flopped down on the bed next to her. "I don't know what it is. It happened in the cell, the first time he touched me. He was naked—"

"Whoah, whoah. He was *naked?*" She said.

"Yeah, or nearly — I made him strip down to his underwear," I said.

"Wait, why?"

"Because I was bored and vindictive. Can I get on with the story?" I said.

Selena laughed. "Please do."

"As I was saying, he was in his underwear, he touched me, and suddenly there was this intense sexual attraction. Like I could feel it radiating off of him, and I felt it to. He smelled my hair, and I wanted nothing more than for him to fuck me against the bars of the jail cell. It was like every cell in my body was calling out to every cell in his."

She raised an eyebrow. "Ace? You're telling me you two have a mating bond?"

"A what?" I asked.

"Like fated mates — that's what it sounds like, at least. Your parts are calling out to his parts, even if your minds or hearts aren't in it. His wolf wants you. Your magic wants him."

"And he wants Tara. And I want to get off this stupid fucking rock," I said, "so who gives a shit?"

"These things are hard to fight. You laugh now, but it'll only get stronger with time. I saw him looking at you. How long can he fight his wolf?"

"Great. Another dangerous guy wants to get his hands on me. What does that make, three?"

"Ace, Ogen, and..."

I looked at her. After Tara and Ace's reaction, I realized I should probably keep it to myself. "Vampire bounty hunter," I said, "working for Faerie King. Remember?"

"Oh yeah. Well aren't you miss popular," she said.

"Oh I'm a verifiable fucking Prom Queen," I said. And she looked at me and laughed.

"You're funny," she said, "I know you probably want to get out of here. But for my sanity? I hope you stay."

I smiled. *I might have a lot of shit headed my way,* I thought, *but it seems like, somehow, I've made a friend.*

"Look, before you go, I've got an idea," she said.

"What's that?"

"There's a beach bonfire tonight. A bunch of townies all getting together. What do you say we crash? Then you can decide if Myston's worth sticking around."

"A party? Really?" I said, raising an eyebrow.

"Sorry — do you not drink? I didn't want to make it awkward," she said.

"Oh no. The first thing I want in the world after a near death experience is a beer — you're just the first one decent enough to offer it. Let's do it."

CHAPTER 15

The beach outside town was a walk from Castle Rock, but we stopped at a convenience store on the way there. The clerk was a goblin fairblood, but he had some kind of illusion charm on to make him seem more human. Selena bought a bottle of wine and a bottle of rum, and we walked the rest of the way to the beach. There was another small lighthouse at the edge of the beach, and this one was sandy, thankfully. The night was cold, and I wore a blue dress that Selena had let me borrow along with my dad's leather jacket. I didn't have the curves she did, but it still clung tightly to my body.

"I feel like a slut," I said as we walked up to the party. The fire burned on the beach, and shadows of young people moved around it, dancing and drinking.

"So? Be a slut! You don't have a man, do you?"

"Not even close," I said.

"Well, if there's one good thing about Myston, it's hot shifters and half vamps. They have them in spades. And looking at you, you'll have your pick. We'll forget all about Ace," she said.

"I don't think I will," I said.

"Oh come on, why?" She said.

"Because he's here."

I placed my head on Selena's chin and turned her head. There, by the fire, Ace and Tara danced. His shirt was open, and she wore a bikini and held a solo cup in one hand. *Fuck*, I thought, *her body rocks.*

I shook the thought away. "Leave it to small towns to invite their sheriff to a party," I said.

"Shit," Selena said, "you sure you wanna go? We can just do girls night instead."

"No, no, let's do it. Like you said — plenty of guys. No reason to dwell," I said.

"Hell yeah. Let's open this wine. There's a jag shifter I've had my eye on…"

We ambled into the party and Selena started introducing me to her friends. I recognized a few: Mae, from Castle Rock, and Grayson, who healed me when I'd washed up on shore. The jag shifter she was crushing on was a tall Black man with close cropped hair and intoxicating golden eyes. He stood shirtless, wearing nothing but a black speedo. I had to stop myself from ogling.

Much to Selena's dismay, the jag shifter — Damien — seemed way more interested in getting into my pants then getting into Selena's. To make it less awkward, I turned to start a conversation with Grayson.

He was handsome as ever, sipping his beer and gazing at the fire. I joined him.

"Need a refresher?" I said.

He snapped out the memory. "Hm?"

I lifted my hand and took his beer. Then, concentrating, I reached for my magic and frosted the beer can over, cooling the liquid within.

He smiled. "Neat trick," he said.

"Not as neat as you stitching me up. I never properly thanked you for that," I said.

"Oh, no that's fine. Being held at knifepoint was thanks enough," he sighed.

"Not every man gets that privilege," I said, "usually, they have to pay."

He arched an eyebrow. "Kinky."

"You don't know the half of it," I said.

He turned to me. "So show me then," he said.

I looked him up and down: same slender frame, blonde hair, underwear model's good looks.

"Something tells me that's not a genuine offer," I said.

He frowned. "And why is that?"

I looked over his shoulder at Ace. He still danced with Tara, drinking deeply from a beer. *Only a shifter could drink beer and still have that six pack.*

"Only the way you were looking at Ace earlier," I said.

He looked over his shoulder at his friend. "Whatever you think you saw..."

"What I saw was a guy who looked like he was in love with his best friend, and was terrified to do anything about it," I said.

His face blanched. He looked over to Ace, making sure he was out of earshot. Then he grabbed my arm and pulled me away from the fire. "How could you think that was remotely cool to do?" He hissed.

I winced. The reproach in his voice was so genuine. *Maybe I shouldn't have led with calling him gay,* I thought.

"Look, I'm sorry — I'm working through some shit," I said.

He scoffed. "Yeah, no kidding," he said, "in the future, when someone extends an olive branch, try not to bring their whole world crashing down around their heads, okay?"

"I don't have a problem with it, obviously! It's 2022, I'm not a hateful person. I was just letting you know what I saw. You're not as discrete as you think. In that way, I was doing you a favor," I said, but I knew it was bullshit the moment I said it.

"Unbelievable," he said, "and for your information, my offer was genuine. It's possible to like both, you know. Although in light of your attitude, I am going to have to rescind my invitation."

Bi, I thought, and the image of me, him, and Ace invaded my mind. *Me pressed between them, watching them kiss...*

I shook the thought away. "I'm sorry. That was really bitchy of me. Can we start over?" I asked.

He sighed. "This will be our second fresh start since we

met. One for the knife at the throat, the other for the knife in the heart."

"Don't be so dramatic," I said.

"You make a man want to be dramatic," he said, "and while we're pointing fingers, I'm not the only one pining after Ace."

I scoffed. "That's absurd — he put me in jail, threw me against the bars—"

"And you liked every second of it," he said, "I know what kind of girl you are. I can smell it on you."

I shivered. *I guess there's no denying it, not to him.*

"So he's hot, so what?" I said, "yeah, a guy with a face like that and the body of a greek god is always going to be hot."

He looked at me, up and down. "No, it's more than that. I'm a shifter, and Ace's best friend — I can feel a mating call from both of you. You're lucky if Tara hasn't spotted it yet. You both reek of pheromones."

I looked over to Ace. He and Tara had moved to playing a game of beer pong.

"What do you say we make them jealous?" I said.

He arched an eyebrow. "How?"

"We pretend to be really into each other. Go dance next to them. You're hot, I'm hot… and I know Ace is hot for me."

"And what would be the point of this?" He said.

I shrugged. "I'm bored and they annoy me," I said.

He considered. "What's in it for me?" He said.

"You get to see if Ace gets jealous. Or at the very least, you help me piss of Tara," I said.

He laughed. "Why would I want to piss of Tara?"

"Because you're in love with her boyfriend, and we both know she sucks," I said.

"She more than sucks. She's a tyrant. And it's stupid to mess with her," he said.

"And…" I said.

He sighed. "And you've got a deal," he said. He extended a hand. I smirked, taking it, and he led me closer to the fire. We found a spot just close enough to where Tara and Ace danced.

His shirt was completely off now, and he held a bottle of whisky in his hand. He seemed drunker than she was, tenderly kissing her neck. She preened like a cat, bathing in the light of the fire.

Grayson looked down at me, eyes bright and serious. He put his big hands on my hips, and I pressed myself to him, grinding against his body with my own. The music seemed to get louder, and the beer and whisky began to cloud my judgement. He raised the bottle to my lips as we danced, and I drank deeply. This went on a for a while, the booze making me looser, sexier. I started unbuttoning his shirt with my teeth — a trick I learned in Miami. I revealed golden skin beneath, the curving mounds of sleek muscle against my tongue. His eyes flashed with fire, and after he raised the bottle to my lips again, he kissed me, the taste of whisky on his soft lips.

I kissed back; he was a good kisser, sure and strong. But through the blonde curls of his hair, I watched Ace dancing with Tara.

Ace watched us back, suddenly becoming very still. Tara still ground against him. But Ace only had eyes for Grayson and I. His eyes flashed gold, briefly becoming those of a wolf. Then he stepped around Tara and marched towards us.

Tara's mouth fell open. "Ace, where are you going?" She said.

But Ace didn't hear her, or if he did, he didn't turn around. Instead, he marched towards us, his shoulders flexed like a dog's hackles.

His wolf was taking over.

He came up behind us, grabbed my waist, smelled my hair. Suddenly I was between them. Grayson and I kept dancing, and I ground against both of their bodies. I felt Ace smell my hair, breathing deeply of my scent. And his scent filled my nostrils, I felt my pupils dilate, felt my heart race. *The mating bond,* I thought.

Grayson, drunk, placed a hand on Ace's arm where it gripped my waist. I could hear Ace growl.

Unthinking, purely animal, he roared and placed a palm in

Grayson's chest, throwing him backwards with inhuman force. Grayson soared through the air, through the crowd, and past Tara, who stared wide-eyed at the scene. Grayson landed in a crouch, disappearing in a flash of fur. Then he stood in his mountain lion form, hissing at Ace.

Ace paid him no mind. He turned me around, his wolf eyes wild, and smelled me deeply again.

The crowd mumbled, staring at us.

"Ace," Tara said, anger fuming in her voice, "Ace!"

Ace's eyes still bore into me, his teeth still bared, his wolf trying to burst through, to take me then and there. As much as I wanted him to, as much as the animal part of me wanted it, I wouldn't let that happen.

You use that perfect cock without my permission, and you lose it, wolf boy.

Tara raised her hand and muttered a spell. Red sparks danced around Ace's head, and his wolf eyes vanished. His face dropped from rage into confusion, and his grip on me loosened.

"What… what happened?" He said. He turned to Tara, who stood, arms folded in her red bikini.

"Babe," he said, "I'm sorry, I couldn't help it! Tara, wait!"

But it was too late. Tara marched away from the fire. Ace followed after her, but she waved her hand behind her, and the fire spread into a wall of flame, blocking his way.

Ace threw his hands up, then buried them in his hair. I stood, flabbergasted. *What just happened?*

I stepped towards him, put a hand on his arm. "Ace…" I said, softly.

"Don't touch me," he said, pulling his arm away. He looked at me with abject hatred, then leapt over the wall of flame, after Tara.

CHAPTER 16

"You okay?" Grayson asked, bounding over to me. He shifted out of his lion form, standing naked before the fire. I averted my eyes.

"Yeah — what was that?" I asked.

He shrugged. "Mating bond. Apparently, Ace's wolf didn't take kindly to us getting friendly. But I guess that's our fault for intentionally trying to agitate them."

"It's our fault he threw you across the bonfire like a ragdoll?" I asked.

He puffed up his chest. "Not like a rag doll, I'd say — did you see that aerial shift? I'd say I looked pretty cool."

"So cool," I said, rolling my eyes.

"Look, he's the alpha of all shifters in Myston. His wolf gets possessive. And for whatever reason, it's possessive of you. I was encroaching on his territory, and his biology wouldn't let that happen."

"So just cause he's the alpha, he gets to be an asshole?" I said.

He shrugged. "Yeah, pretty much," he said.

"That's stupid. And he might be the alpha, but Tara has him completely whipped," I said.

Grayson frowned, looking to where Ace and Tara had disappeared. "Lets hope he managed to patch it up. Tara can be downright scary when she's jealous."

"She's scary all the time," I said.

"Fair," he said, "so…what do we do now?" His eyes traced up and down my body. *He's gone something on his mind, and it's not just fake dancing.*

"I don't—"

"Ana!" Selena said, running towards me. She dragged Damien behind her. "What the hell was that?"

I sighed. Selena seemed drunk, trying to keep it together. "No idea," I said, "Ace was drunk, I guess."

"That looked like some serious alpha wolf aggression, not just the case of the missing six pack," she said, arching an eyebrow.

"It's fine, I think I'm just going to head home," I said.

Selena frowned. Damien stood behind her, his big hands on the bare skin of her stomach. "Oh… Okay, I'll go too," she said, but I could tell she didn't want to leave.

"No, no, it's fine. It's not a far walk to Castle Rock. You stay," I said.

"You sure?" She said.

"I'll walk her," Grayson said. He stepped towards me and put a protective hand over my shoulder.

"No, I— I think I'd rather be alone," I said.

He frowned. "It's late, and you've been drinking. Please, let me—"

"No, Grayson," I said, "I'm gonna go."

His mouth dropped open, as if he were about to speak, but instead he just took his arm off my waist. "Okay," he said, "well, I'll — I'll see you around."

I nodded. Selena looked from me to Damien. "I'll be back later tonight," she said, "we can dish."

I smiled, waved, and walked away from the bonfire.

The sounds of the party disappeared behind me. The music turned back on after the scene with Ace and Grayson, and the party goers slowly returned to silhouettes on the shore. Half a mile down the beach, the music and fire was replaced by lapping waves and moonlight, and she was alone. She pulled her dad's jacket tight around herself, but it barely covered her legs. Cold wind whipped off the lake in gusts.

What is Ace's problem? He wants me, demands me, and then hates me for it — can't he just leave me alone?

But I knew that I was just as guilty — I goaded him when I knew he couldn't handle it.

And you used Grayson to do it, I thought. Maybe I deserved all the bad people hunting me — it would seem that even despite my best intentions, I couldn't keep from leading them on. *I'm a curse,* I thought, Tara's words echoing in my mind. It hurt because I knew it was true. I always knew, deep down, that whoever came for my family the night they died was there for *me.* I remember his inhuman voice, saying: *Where is she?*

Who else could the man have been talking about?

You killed your family. Your mother. Your brother. Your father. And you'll kill everyone on this island, if you stay here. You know it's true.

A sound.

It came from behind me, a whisper of a padded foot on the sand.

I whipped around, peering into the night.

"Ace?" I called, "Grayson?"

But even with the moonlight, I couldn't see far from the lake; the pine trees crowded the shoreline, looking like ragged teeth piercing the night.

I summoned light from my hand; it glowed from ice crystals that formed in the air, a constellation of luminous snowflakes.

Another sound, this one, northward on the beach. I turned around again.

A wolf stood on the shore, head lowered, teeth bared. It was pure black, except for its golden eyes and white, bared teeth. *That's not Ace,* I thought.

Then, behind me: another growl. I could feel a second wolf shifter at my back, stepping towards me.

My panic fought against the liquor in my veins. I raised

my hands, drawing water from the lake. It floated towards me, whipping in riptides, forming a defensive ring between the wolves and I.

"What do you want?" I asked. But I already knew. *Ogen's pack,* I thought, *they found me.* I concentrated, bringing down the temperature of the water. It expanded into wicked spikes, ready to strike at the wolves' hearts.

Then, a flash of light. Fire seared my hands, evaporating the defensive ring of ice. My wrists were suddenly bound in rings of fire, as were my legs. I fell, sent off balance, to the sand.

I looked up, blowing hair out of my face.

And Tara stood above me, between the two wolves, magic shining around her hands.

"You know, at first, it wasn't personal," she said. "But now I'm going to enjoy this. I told you to stay away from my boyfriend."

CHAPTER 17

Tara stepped towards me. Flame whispered through her fingers, beckoning my magical restraints to tighten. I forced myself onto my knees. The wolves crept towards me, still growling.

"You're working with Ogen? You?" I said.

She looked down at me, firelight flickering in her eyes. "It's the right thing to do," she said.

"Right thing to do? Hunting me, kidnapping me, wiping my memory — all of that was the right thing to do?"

"You don't understand the danger you pose. Ogen did. That's why we did what we did," she said.

"*We?* You mean you're the one who wiped my memory?" I said.

"It was the only way," she said.

"Only way to do *what?* This doesn't make any sense — Ogen kidnaps me, but then tries to kill me. I escape, you find me, you rescue me from the Wendigo. What kind of fucked up game are you playing?"

"This isn't a game. This is about keeping everyone safe. About keeping Ace safe. You are a threat to everything I love — to the whole world," she said.

"I promise you, I don't understand any of this. I'm not working with Farien. I just want to leave," I said.

"I know you don't understand. That doesn't mean you

aren't dangerous," she said.

I exhaled. My magic pushed against her restraints, but they responded my tightening, burning the skin around my wrists. I gasped, hissing at the pain.

"So what now? You think killing me will make Farien very happy? How do you know he won't want revenge?" I said. Maybe it was a stupid thing to say, but I was running out of options.

She smiled. "Not yet. That will fall to Ogen," she said.

"Are you basically telling me I have to speak with your manager?" I said.

She sighed. "Always with the quips. And look where that got you," she said.

I shrugged. "Ace seems to like it."

Smack.

Tara's hand slapped across my face, sending sparks flying. Pain seared across my face, and my head jerked to the side.

"You don't say his name," she said.

Blood dripped from my lip. "Oh, sorry. Should I just call him daddy? Or is that just for you?"

Tara's eyes widened, then narrowed. She let out a scream and raised her fist, summoning a ball of flame. She brought it down against my cheek; I could feel the heat of her spell singeing my hair.

And then, nothing. A weight swept my side, and a feeling of fur, of muscle.

And when I opened my eyes, I was laying in the sand ten feet away from Tara. And Ace's wolf was standing between Tara and I, teeth bared.

"Ace," Tara said.

Ace slowly shifted back to his human form. He stood, naked, chest heaving, standing over me. Tara's two wolf cronies stepped towards him, rearing on their hind legs, ready to pounce. Tara raised a hand to stop them.

"Baby," she said.

"What are you doing?" He whispered. "Who are these goons?"

Tara smiled softly. "These are Ogen's pack members."

Ace's face twisted in confusion and anger. "What are they doing on the island? You brought them here?"

"We have the same goals, Ace. Ogen wants what's best for the island. For us," she said, stepping forward.

"How can you say that? He's a monster, he's a tyrant—"

"He's the only thing standing between us and Farien," she said, "the only one with enough power to stop him. He's learned things, in the Fae — powerful things. But he needs Ana's power to open the gate to the Fae and bring his army through. And once the rest of his forces cross over from the Otherworld, he can defend Myston."

Open the gate to the Fae? I can't do that.

"He can rule Myston, you mean," Ace said.

"Sometimes protection and control go hand in hand," Tara said, "you of all people should know that." Her eyes dropped, heavy lidded, lashes batting.

"I never wanted to control you," he said, "if anything, you controlled me."

"I protected you," she spat, "from whores like her. From making a fool of yourself. I made you sheriff; I made you what you are."

Ace closed his eyes. "You and me are through, Tara," he said.

Her eyes narrowed. "You don't mean that," she said.

"I do," he said.

"Is it only for her?" She said.

Ace looked over his shoulder at me, laying in the sand. He turned back to Tara, but said nothing.

"I see," she said. She put her hands at her sides and summoned blood-red twists of magic around them. "I'm sorry, Ace. But I need to protect my town."

Tara turned to the wolves at her side. "Jax, Alec. Take her."

The wolves lunged. Ace shifted into his wolf form in an instant, but the brown wolf closed its jaws around his leg. He howled and snapped, tearing off the brown wolf's ear. Blood sprayed across the shore, and the wolf jerked away, cowering, tail between its legs. Ace's wolf dropped the ear just as the black wolf struck him from the side. Ace toppled, and the wolf's teeth and claws tore his flesh. Blood and fur sprayed.

"Ace!" I cried. I fought against the magical restraints, but they only tightened, burning my already charred skin.

Tara looked on, her face unreadable: disdain? Panic? Sadness? I thought I saw a tear shine on her face, but who could say?

Ace howled again, snapping at the black wolf's neck. He snapped down, found his footing, and jerked his head. The wolf flew to the side, skidding in the sand. But the brown wolf had found its courage, and jumped onto Ace's back, clamping its teeth. Ace sank into the sand, bleeding. The black wolf limped back to him, teeth bared.

He's going to die, I thought, *she's going to let him die.*

Ace howled again, weaker this time. The black wolf leapt, teeth aiming for his exposed belly.

"*No!*" I screamed.

Magic welled up inside me; blue wisps of light left my skin, floating into the moonlight. And to my left, the water of Lake Superior began to glow cerulean blue. The fire-ropes around my wrists and legs fizzled out, overwhelmed by cold power. Rage filled me, looking at the wolves that crowded Ace's prone form.

My knees left the ground; wind whipped around me, and I floated, my power overwhelmingly bright.

"*Leave. Him. Alone!*" I screamed.

The water of the lake rose around me, a tidal wave of water and light. I raise my hands, and the wave crashed, striking the two wolves with icy power. Tara, too, vanished in the swell. The wave swept into the woods, toppling trees and throwing stones. The wave swept onward, the roar of water deafening.

I dropped to the ground, my magic leaving me.

The world went dark.

CHAPTER 18

I woke in the dark; feeling sore all over. Memories of the battle swirled, of Tara's magic burning me, of Ace rescuing me. Of a tidal wave of glowing blue water. The world vanishing, and then…

Grabbing his fur; Ace nudging me onto his back. Limping into the woods, his wolf leaving a trail of blood behind it. Fading in and out of consciousness. And then…

My eyes adjusted to the dark. I lay on a pile of old blankets on a stone floor. I looked around, and saw that I lay in a cave. Stalactites dripped from the ceiling, and warped stone walls curved around me, dripping with moss. At the entrance, wind whipped and rain thrashed, sending gusts of fragrant storm into the recesses of the cave. Lightning flashed, followed quickly by thunder, and I saw the body of Ace's wolf laid out in the stone. Unmoving.

"Ace!" I cried. I crawled towards the wolf, forcing myself forward on the stone, army crawling. His wolf's body was cold. And then, a slight rise of the creature's chest. A shattered breath.

He's alive.

I placed my hands on his stomach, where a gaping, crusted wound sat. Red blood dripped onto the cave floor. With my other hand, I drew rain from the outside storm, drawing all the storm's power with it. It came to me and I could see flashes of lightening trapped in the stream of water. I brought the water to Ace's wound, concentrated, and pushed my magic into him.

A howl pierced the night. Ace's wolf's head whipped up, letting out a growl. He snapped up, onto his four feet, and suddenly was behind me, teeth bared, a snarl on his face.

I raised my hands to placate him, but the sight of the angry wolf made me shudder.

"You're hurt," I said.

Ace's wolf looked at me, eyes widening. Its snarl vanished, and it limped forward, digging its snout into my hair. It inhaled deeply, taking in the scent of me. He grumbled, then collapsed to the ground, into my arms. The creature let out a pathetic whimper. I saw then the rest of the wounds: deep gashes and claw marks and bites, tearing away fur and flesh, revealing bone.

He almost died for me, I thought, *and even with his shifter healing factor, he might still die. I need to do something.*

I summoned more water from the storm, healed another gash. But just as it sealed shut, my magic flickered out. The glowing water faded, splashed to the cave floor. *I'm spent. Whatever I did with the tidal wave, it took all the magic I had.*

I looked at Ace, dying in front of me. *No! I won't let him die!*

I looked around the cave; it seemed as though it was previously inhabited. Besides the blankets were I slept, there were crates of supplies tucked into corners. Oil lamps and candles sat tucked into stone corners, dark. I moved to them, grabbed a box of matches, and brought light into the cave. They flickered weakly against the gusts of wind that snuck into the cave mouth.

I moved to the crates that stood near the cave entrance. There were weapons — a few pistols, knives — and foodstuffs, cans of soup and dried beans. *It's a bugout shelter,* I thought, *smart. He must have known one day he'd need it.*

I frowned. That meant there must be first aid around the cave somewhere. I tore through boxes and crates until I found a small red box with a white cross on the cover. I ran to Ace, ripping open the box. Inside were needles, gauze, medicine…

Fuck! I wouldn't know how to use this on a human. How the

hell am I supposed to use it on a wolf?

"You're gonna be okay," I whispered, "can you shift back to human form?"

Ace's wolf looked up at me with tired golden eyes. He shook his head.

He's too injured. Shifting back would be too risky.

I closed my eyes, picked up the needle, and began to stitch.

Ace's wolf snapped at me, teeth bared.

"What? I'm trying to help!" I said, but I still felt bad. "Hold still. Baby."

His wolf set his head down, allowing me to continue stitching.

After a painful half four of clumsy stitches, I had finally finished the major wounds. I put antiseptic on it, per the instructions in the first aid manual, and bandaged what I could. *Now all there's left to do is wait.*

Unsure what else I could do, I tried to start a fire. My fire making skills were non-existent, and my fire magic skills were even worse — the curse of being a water witch. Eventually, after an hour of trying and the complete box of matches, I got a small fire going. The cave lit up, and I saw the cave paintings shimmering on the wall. I moved towards them. They were pictographs, I realized, carved into the stone by the First Nations. I saw wolves turning into men, women with magic flowing from their hands, and beasts drinking human blood. *I guess supernaturals always liked this island.*

Above them all, shrouded in darkness, was a single figure. He had black eyes, pale skin, and flowing white hair. His robes were blue, and all around him were legions of wolves and winter beasts. Ice and frost spread from his feet, causing famine and disease wherever he walked.

And I knew him.

Farien, the Winter's King.

Hello, dear, I thought. But I shivered, looking at his black eyes. How could I be fated to something like that?

I looked back to where Ace's wolf slept on the floor. *Am I though? If Farien is truly my fated mate, what is thing I feel with Ace?*

I shook the thought away and started to cook: beans and rice, prepackaged. Old military food. Unsurprisingly, Ace's wolf wouldn't eat. Not raw meat, I guessed. I ate some, but found I didn't have much of an appetite after stitching up Ace. *If he doesn't eat, he won't have the strength to heal.*

The thought worried me, but as the storm railed outside, I was lulled again into sleep.

I curled up next to Ace's hulking wolf form, feeling the warmth from his fur meet the warmth of the fire. Then, in an instant, I slept.

I dreamed.

I sat on the shore again. This time, it was winter, and icebergs floated in the water. Ahead of me, a familiar face rose from the depths. Alabaster white skin, black eyes, flowing dark hair. He was naked, and I watched the cruel edges of his muscles curve like ice. His face was perfect, more beautiful than the most beautiful vampire. All sharp angles and soft skin, perfect plump lips just made for biting. I lay back on the beach and felt my legs open as he stepped towards me. He was more slender than Ace, more lithe, but taller and broader. He must have approached seven feet in height, all of it immaculately carved like a marble statue. I followed the ridges of his stomach muscles to the arrow of his adonis belt, to the patch of pubic hair that hovered above a pale, erect cock. It was perfect and smooth, massive. I looked at it with trepidation, biting my lip, but my legs opened wider. My pussy was slicked over with warm water like spring rain, and I realized I was naked too, my breasts exposed against the cold air. My nipples were pink candies against pale skin, painfully tweaked. I reached up and twisted one with a finger. With my other hand, I pressed a finger against my clit, rubbing the wetness there.

My lord stepped towards me. My king. I could feel his power overwhelming me.

"My mate," he said, and his voice was low and sonorous as a midnight storm.

"My king," I gasped.

He knelt in the snow and the sand and opened my legs. His hands were like ice, and I gasped at his touch. When he pressed the head of his cock against my warm pussy, I could feel the coldness of it, a spear of ice.

"I will fuck you here," he said, "and you will bear my son. And together, we will bring the mortal realm to its knees."

He plunged his cock into me. I could feel the iciness of it mix with the warm wetness of my hole, and he roared, unloading himself into my womb—

I woke with a gasp.

The cave was dark; the fire had dimmed to cinders. I felt behind me for Ace, but didn't feel his wolf. *What was that dream? Why did I want that… that monster to fuck me so badly?*

"Bad dreams?" A voice said from behind me. I whipped around, expecting another fight. Instead, I saw Ace, in his human form, leaning against the cave wall. He'd dragged himself over, leaving a trail of blood; messy stitches popped out of reopened wounds. His face was grey and haggard.

He coughed, and I could see red blood dribble at his lips.

He's dying.

CHAPTER 19

"Ace," I breathed. I moved over to him, placing a hand on his shoulder. He was naked, covered in blood and dirt. His blue, human eyes looked up at me with... what? Admiration? Fear? Kindness?

"It's not so bad," he said, coughing again, "I've had worse."

"Really?" I said, wincing.

He coughed again. "No, no. This is pretty fucked."

I smiled. "Yeah, it is," I said, "here, let me..." I reached for the first aid kit.

"Ana — with all due respect for saving my life, your medicine skills could use some work. Any chance you have some magic left?"

I frowned. I raised my hands to a bite mark on his shoulder, drawing water from the air. It shimmered, absorbing into the wound. The bite mark vanished, healing back into tanned skin. He sighed with relief, and I tried not to let him see the effort it took me. I wiped sweat from my forehead.

I moved to the next wound — a nasty, crusted gash on his obliques. I touched the skin there, to find it was hot. *Infection.* I thought. The stitches I'd tried to put in were a bloody mess after he shifted back to human form. I took scissors from the first aid kit and slowly removed them, Ace trying not to flinch with pain every time I did. The wound was red and angry, and white puss leaked from the wound. *If this doesn't heal, the infection could move to the blood. He'll be dead in a day.*

I raised my hands to the wound, gathering magic — but none came. The wound sat festering, as I sat powerless.

Tears stung my eyes. "I— I'm sorry," I said.

He looked at me with his big blue eyes and smiled weakly. "Hey, hey— it's okay. You tried. You helped heal me. I'll get better, I promise."

"No," I said, tears falling freely, "I'm sorry I ever came here. Tara is right, I'm a curse. I hurt everyone I touch. And now you…"

His face winced a I mentioned Tara's name.

"I did what I did to protect you. I made that choice. It's not your fault that Ogen and Tara and whoever else is chasing you. You're innocent in this, Ana," he said.

"She said… she said that Ogen needed my power to open the gate to Fae, and let his army through. Do you know anything about that?" I said.

He shook his head. "No clue. Tara always handled the heavy magic stuff. I was more of a fight first, ask questions later kind of guy. But I know you're powerful. It makes sense that Ogen might need your power to do something like that."

"I can't open the gate to the Fae! I can barely control my powers as is!" I said.

He frowned. "You're stronger than you know, Ana. I believe you can do anything. But if Ogen wants you, it's important he never gets his hands on you. Tara might think he plans to protect Myston, but he wants to rule us. I can feel it. He's a tyrant, and he won't stop until he rules the whole supernatural underworld. Starting with my home town."

"What are we going to do?" I said, "Tara and Ogen are still out there. How did they even get on the island? I thought Ogen was on the mainland. And that no one could get through without the people of the island letting them."

"Tara is the mayor, remember? She must have let them on. If my hunch is right, Ogen has been on the island for a while," he said.

"What do you mean?" I said.

"Do you remember when you first washed up? I said it was impossible for you to just wander through the wards around the island?"

"Yeah, so?" I said.

"What if you didn't wander through? What if Ogen was keeping you prisoner *on* Myst Isle?" He said.

I thought back to the night I escaped from him. Running through the woods, to the shore… I thought I'd left the mainland and washed up on Myston's beach, but what if I'd just moved to another part of the island?

"That doesn't make any sense — that would mean…"

"That his whole pack is here. He's already set up his base of operations somewhere in the Mistwood. There's hundreds of square miles of forest down there. Tara must have been letting them through the islands defenses. Hell, maybe Ogen even crossed over the Fae right here on Myston. This is his old home, after all."

I stopped. It would make sense; if Tara really was working with Ogen, if she really was the witch that wiped my memory… she could have let them establish a base somewhere on the island.

"That would mean…" I started.

"That Ogen is somewhere on the island, with his whole pack, and is probably looking for us right now," he said.

"Fuck."

"Fuck is right," he said.

"What do we do? Does anyone know about this cave?"

He shook his head. "No — I kept this one in my back pocket, just in case."

"Not even Tara?" I said, not wanting to upset him.

He looked at me, almost guiltily. "I never told her. I figured… well let's just say I'm not a complete idiot. I knew something was going on with her — I just never thought she would try to kill me."

"So we have a little time. But they're still coming for us," I said.

He nodded towards the rain outside. "The storm will disperse our sent, make us hard to track. I have a few magical wards around the place that I managed to buy off witches in town, but I don't know how good they are. They can keep us safe for a few days, I think."

He winced again, and I saw that one of his wounds had opened back up.

"We might not have a few days," I said. Tears flooded my eyes, making it hard to see.

"Don't talk like that," he said.

"I'm so sorry. It's all my fault, and now we're going to die in a fucking cave," I said.

"It's not your fault, I told you. It's Tara's, for tricking you. For tricking both of us," he said.

I looked outside, at the storm. "Maybe she's right," I said.

"Ana, no—"

"Farien wants me. That's the cause of all of this. If he comes for me, that could mean the end of the world as we know it. Death and destruction, right? Winter that never ends? No matter where I go, that's what I'll bring: death."

"That's not true!" He said.

"But you still got hurt protecting me. I should have left the moment I knew," I said.

He frowned. "I didn't want you to go," he said, "I'm glad you stayed."

I looked down at him. His grey face, his bloodied body.

"Ace..." I said.

"I'm so glad you stayed," he said again. His hand slipped on to mine, and I felt the clamminess of it. I put a hand on his forehead, feeling the fever. Then I let my hand slip onto his face, cupping it.

His other hand rested on the small of my back. I felt that force moving between us, an invincible tide. I looked into his eyes and saw endless oceans there. His lips parted slightly, and I found that I was leaning forward.

My eyes closed.

Our lips met.

His taste was salt and blood; his stubble scraped against my cheeks. Lips parted and met again, wetness and warmth spreading through me, arousal taking root in my belly.

I pulled back, not wanting to hurt him. He winced.

"I...I—"

"I didn't want to die without getting to try that," he said, weakly.

Despite myself, I laughed. I pressed my forehead to his, letting tears fall on his face. "You're not going to die here, Ace," I said, "not if I can help it."

I stood, wiping away the tears.

"Where are you going?" He said.

I moved to the entrance of the cave, where the storm raged outside.

"To save your life," I said.

And get the magic I need to do it.

* * *

Ace called weakly after me, but I ignored him. I stepped out of the cave, feeling icy rain plaster my face and hair. Thunder shook my bones, and lightening briefly illuminated the grey-blue sky. Dark pine trees stood sentinel around the cave, leaving beds of orange pine needles on the floor.

I didn't waste any magic keeping the cold rain from me. Instead, I let it soak my hair and clothes, making my jeans stick to pale skin, and dark hair to tanned face. I marched forward, pushing against the storm, wind gusting me and cutting through my ruined party dress like knives. I clenched my arms tightly, teeth chattering, and marched through the woods.

The pine trees fell away into shrubs and dunes, and suddenly I was standing on the lake shore. To my right, the beach vanished into grey mist. To my right, downed pine trees bobbed in the water, reaching like skeletal hands. The stones under my feet were ancient and speckled like dinosaur eggs, slicked with rain.

The lake stretched out before me, endless and ancient. Wind whipped up white waves that crashed onto the shore and sent sprays of liquid onto me, chilling me to my core. The dress became too soaked, and it only made me colder, so I pulled it off my skin, peeling it off like a snake. I tossed it to the side, and the waves lapped it up, taking it out to sea. Above, the storm raged, flashing in arcs of pure power, purple lightening illuminating my naked body. Goose bumps speckled my pale skin like an egg, and I raised my arms to the storm.

"I'm not afraid of you!" I shouted. The storm boomed back in defiance.

The next time lightning flashed, a memory came back to me in waves. *My mother, sitting by the river, the roar of a waterfall before us. "Magic is everywhere," she said. She closed her eyes and listened to the water move, her hand in mine. I looked up at her, her brown hair flowing in rivulets down her back. "Magic is everything. The word we use, Magic, is limited. We see it as separate from technology, from the physical world, from electricity or the energy of the sun. But there is only one Power. All power comes from Creation. It is the same Power that allows shifters to shift. It is the same Power that vampires take from their victims; it is the same power that flows through the dams downriver, and powers our home. The power that makes trees grow old and strong. The power that God used to create the world, that the Old Gods used to shape it to their will. And this is the Power that witches wield."*

"I thought the Power came from me?" I said, fingers in my mouth. Already, I was using magic, even at nine. She smiled. "It does come from you — but you are limited. The world is not. If you ever need more of it, in dire emergencies only, you can ask the world for more. You are a water witch, and so the forces of your element will come to your aid. The storm, the sea, winter, the roar of rivers... beseech them for their aid, and they may let you borrow it... but beware. The Power destroys as well as creates. Use it wisely."

Her mother closed her eyes and raised her hand. Before them, the waterfall began to glow with sea-green light. The light flowed from the river and into her mother, and her mother sent the magic back as a flurry of ice. Then the waterfall, slowed, and stopped, frozen in time, and the valley was quiet.

"I beseech you!" I screamed, "I beseech the power of the storm and sea! My mate is dying! Gift me the power to heal him!"

I raised my arms, reaching for the sky. At first, nothing happened. Then, I felt a slow, cold power seep into me. Blue light wiped from my skin, swirling like a whirlpool.

"More!" I shouted, "I need more!"

The sky boomed in response. Lightening flashed over the lake, and a winter wind swept towards me, freezing the water on my skin.

"Please!" I shouted.

Then, above me, a rumble. I looked to the storm clouds gathering there, deep purple and gray like dead skin. In the clouds, I thought I saw a face: a man's face, pale, with dark eyes.

Lightening flashed.

It arced towards me, crawling out of the sky in slow motion. When the lightening struck me, the whole world exploded into light.

Power. Surging through every cell in my body.

I gasped, but I didn't need air. The storm raged inside me, bursting at my fingertips. I hovered above the ground, blue power radiating off of me, lightning crackling in my hair. It was overwhelming, but I knew I couldn't hold it for long. *It's too much power. It will slip away. I need to get to Ace.*

I turned to move towards him, but I didn't need to move. The beach vanished, and I flickered into existence back in the cave.

Ace was beneath me, awash in the light of my power.

His eyes widened weakly, his skin grey and drained of blood. He clutched his side, where his largest wound still bled.

You will not die, I thought, *you will be strong.*

And I floated down to him, placing my lips on his. The power of the storm flowed out from me and into him.

Suddenly we were both in the air, both of our skins awash in blue light. His back arched as if in pain, and his arms shot out to the side. I placed a hand on his wound and poured power into him; I felt it seal beneath my touch, felt his skin become hard and strong.

Then the last of my power left me, and we fell. Ace caught me in his arms, standing strong. He looked down at me with worried eyes, and I saw that they still glowed blue, power streaming from them.

In a voice drenched in power, he said my name.

"Ana..."

CHAPTER 20

I awoke again, laying on the pile of furs and blankets. I was still naked, but Ace had covered me with a blanket. He knelt before the fire, stoking it. As I opened my eyes, I noted that his wounds had completely healed: there weren't even scars to hint that he'd once been near death. His skin was back to a golden tan, the grey vanished, and his eyes were serious and bright, no longer haggard and bagged.

I pushed myself up on one arm. To my surprise, I didn't feel worn out. I felt... good. Powerful. Remnants of the storm's power still lurked in me, thunderous.

"Ana!" Ace said, standing. He wore nothing but jeans, lying low, beneath the V of his abdomen. He moved over to me, put a hand on my shoulder. "You should rest; don't move too fast."

"No, I feel fine, really. What happened?" I said. The memories of the storm were vague, shrouded in blinding light.

"You absorbed the power of the storm. Then you came back, and healed me," he said. "Look!"

He ran his hands down his abs, then turned around and showed his muscular back. "Not a scratch on me. And I feel great! Watch this."

In a flash, he leapt at the wall, shifting mid air into his wolf form. The wolf bounded around the cave, running along the wall, and then leapt and shifted back into Ace. He landed in human form in a crouch. "I've never shifted that fast. Whatever you did to me — I feel better than I have in years."

There is only one Power, she thought.

"I feel it too — I absorbed the storm, and must have given a good amount of that power to you. My mother used to say that all magic is the same. It can be transferred between vessels: people, objects, nature. I guess when I healed you, I supercharged you too."

Ace stood. To my surprise, he still wore his jeans.

"Wait — shouldn't you have ripped out of those when you shifted?" I said.

He shrugged. "I've known some powerful shifters who can shift their clothes with their bodies — but those shifters are centuries old. Ogen is one of them — he wears armor to battle, and shifts it to fit his wolf. He has magic as well as shifting abilities."

I breathed. "And now, I guess, so do you," I said.

Ace thought for a moment. He looked like he was about to say something, but was too nervous.

"What is it?" I asked.

"Tara used to talk about power transfer. She said there were a few ways it could happen... vampires can do it by feeding. Killing is one way to absorb another being's magic. There are rituals that can transfer magic, too... but she said there was another way."

"What's that?"

He looked uncomfortable. His hand rubbed his neck, exposing a toned underarm and hairy pit. "Love," he said, looking at me with ice-blue eyes.

My voice caught in my throat.

"I...I—"

"You don't have to say anything. I don't know if that's the case. But I know if there's a love bond, power can sometimes flow freely between two mates."

"For that to be true, it would have to go both ways," I said.

He shrugged, looking at me. "Then I guess it can't be true," he said.

I frowned. *Of course. There's no way he could love me. But do I love him?*

"Did you and Tara ever exchange power?" I asked, trying to change the subject.

He shook his head. "If we did, it was never much. She could shift because of her bond to me, but I never absorbed much of her magic."

"Does that go away, now that you two are…"

"Broken up?" He said, "I don't know how that works. I guess the love would have to go away."

"Did it?" I asked.

"Does it ever?" He said.

We were silent for a moment. He came towards me slowly. Suddenly, the thrum of magic between us was palpable.

"I need to know," he said, "do you feel it too?"

My mouth opened, ready to deny it. But as I looked at him, his perfect face flickering in the firelight, his blue eyes preternaturally bright, I simply couldn't.

"Ever since the first day in the cell," I said, breathlessly.

"I nearly took you right there. My wolf was begging me to," he said. His voice was suddenly a low growl.

"Why didn't you?"

"Because I am a loyal person. I am not an animal. I would never betray my mate," he said.

Perhaps the sexiest quality in a man, I thought.

He continued. "… but I don't have a mate anymore."

I looked up at him. His eyes were serious, nearly glowing with power. His muscles were tensed, his fists clenched. I remembered those hands around Tara's throat as he shoved her against the lighthouse wall.

"Where does that leave us?" I asked.

As if in answer, I could see his cock swell in his jeans. It was massive, extending down halfway to his knee. He knelt, and brought his face close to mine.

"Be my new mate, Anastasia Walker," he said.

"What? That's insane — we barely know each other," I said.

"And yet your blood calls to mine. I can smell it on you; I can smell your pussy getting wet right now," he said. He took a deep breath, and his eyes flashed golden. "You are my fated mate, Ana."

The magic between us pulled again; I wanted nothing more than to dive into his arms, to feel him inside me. But I resisted, thinking of the dark god in my dreams.

"What about Farien?" I asked, "he seems to think that I am destined for him. If he finds out, he will kill you. Destroy everything you love."

His face twisted into a snarl. "Let him try; you are mine. I will kill anyone who lays a finger on you."

His voice a growl. "I will protect you to my dying breath; you will bear my children, be my bride, and will never want for anything again. I will give you anything you want. I will show you complete and utter devotion. All you need to do, is say yes."

His eyes bore into me, unblinking.

I leaned forward, unable to resist any longer. He leaned in too, mouth open.

I stopped him, placing a finger on his lips. He looked at me, confusion and anger swelling in his face.

"Prove it," I said. And I pointed a finger downwards, opening my legs.

He looked down, understanding dawning. He licked his lips, then, like a man praying, slowly lowered himself down. "Yes, ma'am," he said.

He brought his face to the warm place between my legs; my pussy was already sweet and shining, like it was covered in liquid sugar. He smelled deeply, moaning as he took in my scent. Then he dove in, nose first, rubbing his face against it. His hips began to grind as he took in my scent, deeper and deeper.

Then, his tongue. He took his first taste, and electricity shot through my body. Fire roared in my belly, pure pleasure. He licked again, lapping like a dog. Hungry, powerful, unrestrained.

I grabbed the back of his head, guided him with his hair. Brown locks caught between my fingers as he growled in pleasure. His huge hands pressed my thighs open even wider, and his tongue flicked my clit slowly. He sucked, kissed, licked; one finger slipped inside, opening me, preparing me for him. I moaned. My head fell back, but I supported myself with his hair. I was so small in his hands, half his size. I watched the muscles of his back ripple in the firelight, saw the storm still raging outside. Lightning flashed, and I could see his jeans slipping down, revealing his ass, two perfect mounds of muscle.

His tongue sped up, flicking greedily at my clit. My pussy lips were soaked, and he reared back and spit on them, rubbing my clit with his rough hand. I could feel an orgasm building in my belly, feel it roar like a wave up my chest, perking my nipples, making my legs shake. "Oh my fucking god," I moaned, "Ace, that's incredible. I want you to fuck me."

His eyes peered up at me, from where he devoured my cunt. He lifted his maw from between my legs, moisture dripping down his chin. I could feel the aggression radiating off of him, watching his muscles bulge and tense with need. And beyond that, our twin magics touching each other. His wolf calling out to my magic, my magic drawing out his wolf.

He dove in and kissed me, hard. His stubble seared the soft skin of my face. Fire roared up me, my pussy calling out as his cock pressed against it. *I need him,* I thought, *fuck, I need his cock.*

He grabbed my arm, so hard I thought it might bruise. Then he picked me up with one hand and laid me on my back, on the furs next to the fire.

"Fuck me already," I moaned, spreading my legs.

"Yeah? You want my cock?" He said.

"Yes, sir, please," I said. And I meant it. I wanted his thick cock in every hole. I wanted him to wreck me.

He looked down at me and grabbed his cock in his fist; it barely covered half of it. Then he slowly slid the tip into me.

I gasped, wincing. *It's too big,* I thought, *I can't take it.*

But then the heat took me; that intense longing of a wolf

in need of a mate. Suddenly my pussy opened up, and he forced himself into me, up to the hilt.

"Fuck!" I screamed, "Oh my god, you're huge."

"Take it," he moaned, "take it all, Ana."

His head dipped back in pleasure. When he looked down at me again, his face was twisted into a wicked grin. "You're going to take my cock, girl. And then when I'm done fucking you, you're going to take my load. No condom. I'm going to get you fucking pregnant."

I whimpered. He leaned forward, thrusting again. Then his huge, strong hand closed around my throat. I gasped. "Don't hurt me," I whispered.

His eyes bored into me, flashing golden. I stared up at the wolf man holding me by the throat. "I would never hurt my mate. But I need to show you that you're mine."

I nodded, and he thrust again into me. I rocked backwards, forced by his hips. *He's too strong*, I thought, *he's a god.*

He thrust again, slowly at first, making me feel every inch of his cock. Then he pulled out again; I could hear the wet sound of him fucking my pussy, feel every bit of friction as he pounded me, feel his pubes grind against my mound. He held my legs open and fucked me freely, grinding into me. I watched his abs writhe as he fucked me, watched his sharp jaw as he smoldered. He said terrible things to me, but that only made me more wet; I was his. I could feel it; my body would never take another mate. His golden skin was dripping with sweat, and the room smelled of skin and sex.

He flipped me onto my knees with his shifter speed; one moment I was on my back, next I was prone, my ass in the air. He shoved his huge cock into me again and I cried out in pleasure. Then he started fucking, slapping my ass with his hands. Red marks covered the jiggling skin where he fucked me mercilessly. When he was bored of my pressing my head into the pillow, he grabbed my hair in one fist and brought my face to his. He whispered, with hot breath, in my ear: "Does that feel good, girl? You like when I wreck your pink little pussy?"

"Yes, sir!" I said, but it came out wobbling as he pounded me again and again.

Then suddenly I was in the air; Ace stood, pulling me up by my thighs. He held me as though I were nothing, a toy. He looked me in the eyes. "Guide my cock into you," he said.

I reached behind me and felt his slick cock, huge and pulsing and hot. I rubbed the tip against my pussy. *I don't know how much more I can take,* I thought, but the moment his cock slipped inside me, I lost all reason. I ground down onto it, letting it penetrate my deepest parts. I could feel him filling me up, taking me for everything I was.

"That's right, good girl," he said, "now grind up and down on it."

I grabbed his shoulders and began to pleasure myself on his cock. He stood, barely working to lift me, his huge hands on my ass. I humped furiously, taking him in and out, in and out, slowly building the burning orgasm. It started between my legs, swelled in my stomach, moved and took all my limbs.

"Fuck, fuck, Ace, I'm coming!" I screamed.

"That's right, come for me baby," he said, "fuck yourself on my cock until you cum."

I squirmed on him. He took my hips in his hands and forced me deeper onto him, over and over. I was nothing to him; lighter than air. He used me like a sex toy, pushing me down on his cock for his twisted pleasure. I moaned, screamed, whimpered as he fucked me without mercy. Finally, his eyes narrowed, and he roared, unleashing his load into me.

I came in that exact moment, feeling his hot seed fill me up. It came with a jolt of magical power, a flash of gold in his eyes. I felt the orgasm spread from my clit to my fingertips, and blue light shone through the cave, crackling like electricity. The storm moved between us, ripe with pleasure.

"Oh, *fuck*," he said, slowing down. He lifted me off of him, set me down on the floor, shaking. I looked up at him, at his hulking form replete with golden muscle. I saw his dripping cock, his cum and my juice still coating it. And I stuck out my tongue and lapped up the mixture, savoring the taste. He shivered as my tongue arced around his tip, sensitive from giving me the greatest fuck of my life.

He grabbed my hair, looked at me in the eyes.

"You are mine, now," he said. And he said it was such certainty that I knew it was true.

He squatted, then lay me back on the furs, gingerly. Like he was handling something precious. I still shook from exertion, from the multiple orgasms that rocked my body. Little aftershocks of pleasure still raced through my limbs, from the sore spot between my legs. He laid down behind me, stuck his nose in my hair, and breathed deeply, inhaling my scent. His muscular arms wrapped around me, his firm chest pressed against my back. I was spent, completely satisfied. I could feel him sleepily kiss my hair, the aggression subsiding. *A kind man. A cruel wolf. Makes for one hell of a fuck.*

"Listen..."he started, "even if you don't love me... and that's okay... I loved you from the first moment I set eyes on you."

I froze. "Ace..."

"Shh. We should rest. Go to sleep, Ana," he said. He kissed my head, hugged me tight, and quickly began to snore.

He loves me? Could that be why some of my power transferred to him?

That would mean that I have to love him too.

Do I?

Can I risk it?

But Tara's voice came back to me: *You're a curse.*

Can you love someone if you put them in danger?

CHAPTER 21

"**S**o what now?" I asked. It was morning, and the storm had passed. The sun rose through the opening of the cave, revealing the wet woods. Birds chirped outside, feasting on worms, and droplets of water glistened on pine needles. Mist rose from the baking Earth, shrouding the island and giving it its name: the Isle of Mist.

Ace knelt by the fire, rekindling it. In the gear he'd stashed in the cave, he kept a camp kettle and a French press for coffee. He'd served me first and produced a protein bar. *Hot, shirtless werewolf making me coffee in the morning. I could get used to this.* He poured himself another cup, then came and draped a blanket over my shoulders. *Right — shifters tend to be pretty devoted to their mates. If that's what we are — how does that work, anyway? One night — even if it was the best sex of my life — isn't going to mate bond us forever, right?*

He leaned against the cave wall and sipped his coffee. "The storm has passed. That means that sooner or later, Ogen and Tara will find us. So we can't stay here."

"Where to, then?" I said, "it's not like we can go back to Myston. Tara is the mayor — what if she has set the whole town against us?"

Ace considered. "She probably has. Maybe even put some magic behind it to really make them believe we're outlaws. But if we wanted to get off the island, we'd have to go through Myston.

And Tara controls the wards. If we left, she'd know, and she'd send Ogen's pack after us."

"So we can't stay here and we can't run. Where does that leave us?" I asked.

"Simple. We fight," he said.

I looked at him; his face was totally serious. "You're joking."

"It's all we can do. We need to be proactive. We get ahead of this thing, and fight, or we die," he said.

"You and I? Versus Ogen One Eye, his pack of wolves, and Tara? Tara is more powerful than I am, and isn't Ogen One Eye like a god?"

"He's more like a demigod. He has a lot of power, but he can be killed," he said.

"Oh cool. And how exactly do we do that?" I said, sarcastically.

"Not by us. We couldn't kill One Eye. But maybe we could send him back to where he came from," he said.

"The Fae?" I said, "and how are we supposed to do that?"

"Tara said that the reason Ogen wanted you is to open the portal to the Fae, so that Ogen can bring the rest of his army through."

"Yeah, but no offense, Tara is kind of fucking crazy. I don't know how to do that! I didn't even know the Fae was real until this week."

"But Tara seems to think you can, and so does Ogen. We know you're more powerful than an ordinary witch. If you can learn to open a portal to the Fae, then maybe I can push Ogen back through it," he said.

I frowned, and tucked a lock of dark hair behind my ear. "Even if I could open a portal, isn't that exactly what Ogen wants? His army will be waiting on the other side, ready to conquer Myston, and then the rest of the supernatural underworld. And if it's not him, we know who else is waiting in the Fae. Farien. And I don't want to risk letting him through."

He frowned. "I don't either. But there has to be a way to

open a portal elsewhere, somewhere Ogen's army or Farien won't get through. I just don't know how. We need help."

"Like, psychological help?" I said.

He smirked. "After last night, probably."

I watched him smile, and heat flushed me. *Daddy issues, here I come,* I thought.

"But no. We need another witch. Someone with more experience than you, who can help us figure it out."

I frowned. "I think I have someone. But you're not going to like it," I said.

* * *

We approached Castle Rock under the cover of nightfall. I rode atop Ace in his wolf form, clutching the fur of his back. I straddled him as he sprinted full speed, the woods blurring around us. Since I infused him with the power of the storm, his wolf seemed even larger and faster than before. *How long will this last?* I wondered. *Surely it can't be forever.*

I kept my eyes on the woods, listening for any sign of a threat. My witch sight illuminated the woods around me, and I saw the magic pulsing in all things: in the Earth, in the trees, even in the mist. Above us, the dome of the sky was interlaced with arcing faerunes. *The island's wards.*

Castle Rock was a beacon of dim light in the darkness; candlelight glowed through the windows of the old fairy keep, and waves crashed against the rocks on its shore. I saw that the castle itself was glowing with faerunes, armored against the outside world. *But will it be enough to keep out Ogen? Tara?*

Ace trotted to a stop. I slipped off his back, hands tracing on his fur. I wore some leftover gear Ace had stored in the cave: jeans, a blue tank top and flannel, and combat boots. Around my waist was an extra holster with a loaded pistol. On the other side, a silver dagger, etched with faerunes. *Useful against shifters. Against Ogen One Eye? Who knows.*

Next me, Ace shifted into his human form. With his new abilities, his clothes shifted with him: he stood in black fatigues, with a similar silver dagger and pistol at his side.

"Okay, I got us here," Ace said, "how do we get inside?"

I looked at the castle; the drawbridge was up, leaving us no way to get inside. Or so it would seem. I stepped towards the coast, raising a hand. Blue light whisped around my hands, streamed from my eyes. I extended it, pushing my magic across the water. Then I lifted it, arcing it above my head. A tunnel opened before me, swirling with blue light; waves of water arced around the edges, and a stone path appeared on the lake's bottom.

Ace raised an eyebrow. "You sure that's gonna hold?"

I smiled. "Afraid of getting wet?"

"You're the one who has to deal with wet dog smell," he said, "but onward we go."

Ace stepped past me and into the tunnel. I followed, curving the water around us as we walked. We moved slowly through the tunnel of glowing water, as fish swam around us, and seaweed was carried by the current. The hull of a sunken sailboat lay on the rocky bottom, just before the gentle rise of Castle Rock's shore.

Ace marched forward, and we exited the lake, stepping onto the island. Before us, the walls of Castle Rock rose into the night sky.

"Can you fly us up there?" He said.

"Can't fly."

"You were like, glowing and levitating earlier."

"I had a bunch of power then. Now? Not so much. Flying is out of the question," I said.

Ace assessed the wall. "I think and can do it. Do you trust me?" He said.

I looked up, then at Ace, smiling. "Always," I said.

Ace closed his eyes, and his features began to shift: he grew taller, and fur sprouted from his arms and face. His muscles swelled, and his face twisted into a half-snout. Suddenly, a half-man beast stood before me, somewhere between wolf and human, yet larger and stronger than both. Ace stood in his hybrid form, golden eyes glowing.

"Climb on," the monster said.

He knelt, and I stepped forward, throwing my arms around his neck. I felt his muscles, his thick fur. A clawed hand gripped my ass, pulling me onto his back. "Hold on tight," he said, his voice a deep snarl. I squeezed his neck, and he shifted into a crouch. Then, with indescribable power, he leapt.

I could feel the cold night air whip around me as we flew through the air. The ground grew smaller, and the ramparts of the castle raced by. I felt a scream building in my throat as we rose.

Ace crashed into the wall, long claws extending. He latched on, digging into the stone, growling to keep from sliding downward. Then he tore a single claw out, placed it a few feet above, and we climbed upward.

We crested the rampart and stood on one of the castle's walls. I slid off of Ace's back, and he turned to face me. I was shaking, terrified from the leap, and he held me in his massive arms, looking down with his golden eyes.

"Don't move," a woman's voice said.

I turned to see a figure standing on the walls, shrouded in shadow.

Then, green light flared around the woman's hands, pulsing into the stone rampart of the castle.

Instantly, the stone at my feet melted, turning liquid. I fell, slipping into the stone. Next to me, Ace sunk too, snarling as the stone swallowed him.

Then the stone became solid again, and I was trapped, only my neck above the surface. My hands were caught, unable to cast.

The shadowy figure stepped forward, into the moonlight.

Selena's face was narrowed into a frown, her brows arched.

"Hello again," she said.

* * *

CHAPTER 22

"You better have a good ass reason for coming back here," Selena said. Ace snarled, fighting against his stone restraints, but it was futile. Green spells twisted through Selena's fingertips. "Ah, ah, ah, wolf boy," she said. She flicked a hand, and both Ace and I slipped into the stone even further. Earth magic; craftier than I thought.

I fought to keep my head above the stone. "Wait! Wait!"

I gasped. "Tara is lying to you. Whatever she said, she's lying! Tara is working with Ogen!"

We stopped slipping as a look of doubt came across her face.

"What did you say?" She said.

"Tara. She's working with Ogen. She thinks that he can save the town," I said. *Leaving out what he needs to save it from, of course.*

"She told me that you killed Ace. You went berserk, she tried to stop you, and then you nearly killed her, too."

"That's a lie! She was the one who attacked Ace," I said.

"Obviously, because he's still alive, and right in front of me," she said.

"Tara must have thought Ace would die, and that she could frame me for the murder," I said, more to myself than to her. *But I healed him, against the odds. So that disproves her lie.*

"She told the whole town. It's a witch hunt out there,

literally," Selena said.

"Yeah, well, she's full of shit," I said, "mind letting us out, now?"

Selena looked between me and Ace. "If I do, will wolf boy calm his shit?"

"Ace?" I said.

He snarled. "I will calm my shit," he said.

Selena nodded. She pressed a hand forward, and green light erupted around me. I rose from the stone, then collapsed. Ace was beside me, shifting back into human form.

"Come on," Selena said, "I need a drink."

Ace and I shared a look, then stood, and followed her into the castle.

* * *

In Selena's bedroom, she poured three glasses of scotch. I realized I shouldn't be drinking, with Ogen probably coming after me that very second, but I needed something to quash the nerves. "So you're telling me," Selena started, "that your new boyfriend's ex-girlfriend — the mayor of this town — is working with a faerie-powered Wolf God to take over the island, all so he can stop some Faerie King from coming to make you *his* girlfriend and plunge the world into a never-ending winter?"

"Well, when you put it like that..." I said.

"It sounds pretty bad," she said.

I sighed, "yeah, it sounds pretty bad. But we have a plan, kind of."

"Which is?" She asked.

I looked at Ace. He shrugged. It was my idea to approach Selena about opening the portal.

"Tara and Ogen seem to think that I can open a portal to the Fae," I said, "and if I really can, then I can send Ogen back to where he came from."

"You want to what... just yeet the Wolf God back to fairyland?" She said.

"I mean, yeah, I guess," I said.

"Okay, I'm in," she said.

I startled. "What?"

"I'm in," she said.

"Well don't you want to… I don't know, don't you want to make fun of us for a dumb plan, or something?"

She rolled her eyes. "Of course I do. But I said we were friends, and I'm loyal to my friends. I'm in."

I stared, open mouthed. *How many people keep their word like that? Solid as a rock, I guess.*

"Okay. Now I just need to figure out how to open the gate," I said, "easier said than done."

She shrugged. "Not really — there's a huge library at Castle Rock. Tara's personal collection, plus the spell books of all the witches and warlocks going back to the island's founding. There's powerful magic down there. What you need is someone who is good with books."

"Like who?" I asked.

Selena smiled. "Like me, dummy. Come on, let's go."

* * *

The library at Castle Rock was a single sprawling tower filled with books; the shelves climbed and leaned over the main space as if they grew there, and tiny witch-lights floated in the air like miniature moons.

I lay on one of the long reading tables, flipping through a book. Truthfully, I was never very good at school. Not a great trait for a witch, when so much could be learned from study and practice. The feel of the spell book, the smell of it, made me nostalgic for my mother. I remembered sitting in her lap, the smell of the pages, her tea steaming beside us. I cuddled up into her wool sweater, trying to read the words along with her, learning each faerune and its purpose. *I miss you, mom,* I thought, *I wish I could go back. Feel that way again, love and be loved so easily.*

"Here!" Selena said, suddenly, "I found it."

I shot up. Ace, who was pacing the room — he wasn't much of a reader, either — darted over to Selena. She had a scroll stretched out before her, nearly the length of the full table.

It looked ancient, almost more like skin than paper. Red ink scrolled faerunes across the page, swirling in circles and lines.

"How do you even read this?" I said, looking at the scroll.

"Patience and time," she said.

"Two things we don't have right now," said Ace.

"I can walk Ana through it; the spell itself is surprisingly simple, it's just impossible to do," she said.

Ace raised an eyebrow. "Impossible? Why?"

"The power it calls for is astronomical. Most witches operate with the power of something like a double-A battery; this spell calls for a nuclear power plant."

Ace frowned and looked over to me. "Can you do that?"

I shrugged, not knowing what to say. "No — I mean, sometimes I have more power than I should. But never for something like that."

"Well, for some reason, Ogen and Tara think you can," Ace said.

I looked at the spell, traced my hand over the runes. *Could I really?*

"I'm still charged from the storm," I said, "but that won't last forever. I can already feel it slipping away."

"Then we need to do it now," Selena said.

"That would involve luring Ogen to us, so we can throw him back in," Ace said, "how are we going to accomplish that?"

I frowned, closing my eyes. "He wants me. So all we need to do is put me somewhere he can get me. Then I'll open the gate, and you two will push him through it."

"Me and wolf boy against Ogen One Eye, Tara, and his whole pack? I don't like those odds," Selena said.

"I can visit my pack mates. Try to get some help. Grayson might be willing, too, if I didn't make him too mad," Ace said.

"Tara told the whole town you're dead and Ana killed you. I don't know how well seeing your friends is going to go," Selena said.

"Worked with you, didn't it?" Ace said, "besides, if push comes to shove, I'm still the Alpha. I can use my Alpha Command

and they'll have to help. Not ideal, but it'll do."

I shook my head. "It still won't be enough."

"It's all we've got," Ace said.

I thought for a moment, then looked to the charm bracelet at my wrist.

Not necessarily.

CHAPTER 23

I stood atop the highest keep of Castle Rock. Here goes nothing, I thought, and I rubbed the snowflake of the charm bracelet between my fingers. It still felt cold to the touch; not painfully cold, just powerfully so. It was filled to the brim with magic, pouring out of it in blue streams.

I put my intentions into the charm, concentrating.

Find me, I thought, *find me here.*

At first, nothing. The sky was dark, shimmering with stars. Dawn was still hours away, and the moon cast wan light over the lake and the ancient stones of the castle. The tower I stood on looked out over the courtyard and the walls of the castle, and far below, waves crashed against stone. The night was cold, and I shivered as the wind bit through my father's leather jacket. A few moments passed, and I thought that he might not come after all.

"Miss me?" A voice said.

I turned around quickly, to see a tall shape standing atop the tower with me. He wore black leather pants and a mesh top, with a long leather overcoat. His eyes were blood red against his pale skin, and his ruby talisman glinted in the moonlight.

"Hardly," I said. I rubbed my arms to stave off the chill; then, not wanting to look weak, I stopped.

"Have you reconsidered my master's proposition?" He said. His voice was smooth as new ice, and it carried a chill. I noticed again how beautiful and refined his face was, white as fresh fallen snow, lips red like blood. *Has he fed recently?*

"I have," I said.

"And?"

"And I won't go with you. I won't go to the Fae," I said.

He blinked, stared, and then scowled. "Then pray tell, why invite me here?"

"You didn't let me finish," I said, "I won't go with you. Unless you help me."

His face shifted from annoyance to intrigue.

"With what task does my lady wish my aid?" He said, smiling.

"Ogen One-Eye is here, on the island. He is coming for me," I said, "I want your help sending him back."

Varnei's eyes flashed with an unfamiliar emotion. *Fear? Anger?*

"Ogen..." he whispered.

"Is that a problem?" I said, "and here I thought my fated mate was an all-powerful Faerie Lord."

"He is. I, however, am not. And Ogen is far too powerful for you — or me — to fight," he said.

"And why is that? What makes him so special?" I asked. The wind whipped around us as if in answer, lending an eerie cast to the dark night.

Varnei sighed. "Years ago, there were four Fae Regents. Farien, the King of Winter. Oberyn, the King of Summer. Larien, Queen of Spring. And Valien, Queen of Autumn. When Ogen came to the Fae, he joined all the packs of Faewolves under one banner. He raided the Spring Palace and slayed the Queen Larien, taking her magic for himself."

I raised an eyebrow. "He can do that? Take a Fairy Queen's magic?"

"Not completely, no — some is always lost. But the ritual he performed stole most of it, and made him nearly a god. He is not as strong as the other Fae Lords, but he is clever, and his army of Faewolves is loyal. We cannot hope to defeat him."

"We won't defeat him. I'll send him back where he came from," I said. I tried to sound confident.

Varnei raised an eyebrow. "You think you're ready to open the gate?"

I paused. *I can't let him use this as an opportunity to let Farien through.*

"I can open it. I think. But only to send Ogen back — not to let anyone through. I need Farien's word that he won't come through the gate."

"And why would Farien take this deal? After all, his express desire is to lay claim to you. When you open the gate, my employer could simply walk through and wage his war against the mortals."

I closed my eyes. "If you do this for me — if you help me send Ogen back to the Fae — then when it's done, I'll return with you."

Varnei froze. "You'll come to the Fae? No questions asked."

I nodded. "Yes," I said.

He smiled. "Well, then. When do we begin?"

In the distance, a howl sounded. It seemed so loud that it shook the trees of the island, made the waves quiver. A flock of crows, startled, launched into he night sky. And on the horizon, a flicker of white in the trees.

"Looks like right now," I said.

CHAPTER 24

I raced down the stairs, Varnei at my heels. Selena ran towards us, down the long stone corridor. "What's happening" she asked, "is that a…"

"Vampire, yeah, long story. Do you have everything for the spell?

Selena looked Varnei up and down, then offered a scroll. "It's all in here. I've got the spell. Let's just hope you've got the juice to cast it," she said.

I frowned. *Could I?* I took the scroll anyway. "So what's the plan?" She said.

"We head to the beach. I lure him there with my scent. Once he's near, I'll need some time to open the gate. You just need to hold them off until them. Once it's open, I'll need to concentrate to keep it that way, so it's up to you three to push him through."

"Three?" Varnei asked, "I count two."

"Ace is coming with his pack — hopefully," I said.

"Ah. The dog."

I ignored the barb. If this was going to work, we would all have to work together.

"Come on. I need to start preparing."

We took the staircase down from the upper floors, then left through the portcullis. Howls pierced the night, and I could feel an oppressive power marching closer. *Ogen.* It struck me just how distinct he felt, like all the magic in the woods and the sea fled from him, rushed past me in an attempt to escape. I marched down the drawbridge, and we took a small stone staircase to the beach. Again, howls in the distance. *They probably already have my scent,* I thought.

"We don't have much time," I said, looking at the scroll, "and the sigils we need to draw look complicated. We should get started."

"Let me see that," Selena said, taking the scroll. Her eyes flickered over the strange circles and faerunes. Then she raised a hand, and sand rose from the beach, swirling in arcs. Green light swept around us like a storm, and symbols began to appear in the earth. Her eyes glowed briefly green, and a wind whipped her hair. Then the sand settled and a huge pentagram lay exposed in the sand, carved from the earth. It glowed for a moment, humming with power, each faerune foreign and crisply drawn. Then the sand flashed, and the runes solidified into green glass, superheated.

Selena dropped her hand and let out an exhausted breath. She wiped a bead of sweat from her forehead. "There. That should save us some time. You really think you can do this?"

Varnei spoke up. "She was, quite literally, born for it."

I looked at him, behind us, leaning against the stone wall of the bridge that lead to Castle Rock. "What's that supposed to mean?" I asked.

He smirked. "Another time," he said, "it looks like our guests are arriving."

I whipped my head towards where Varnei pointed.

A huge white wolf pounded down the beach, tracked by a small army of shifters. It was close enough to see its one missing eye.

Ogen.

A whooshing sounded over head. Varnei landed in front of me in a crouch. He stood slowly, and I noticed that he'd lost his overcoat and shirt. He stood in the moonlight bare chested, and for the first time I saw his intricate tattoos. They spiraled around his arms in bands interspersed with blocky faerunes, inked in blood red. His back was set with a series of v-shaped patterns, finished with circular pentagrams along his spine. Muscles rippled under the tattoos, as if made of marble. He was sleeker than Ace, more lithe, and I watched as the muscles of his lower back dipped into his low-riding leather pants. The curves of perfectly tight asscheeks just hinted over the waist. *Whoah*, I thought.

Ogen slid to a halt on the beach, nose raised in the air. His pack slowed as well, snarling, fangs bared. Then, from Ogen's wolf-mouth, he spoke. "Leech," he growled, looking at Varnei. "Step aside."

"Since you asked so nicely," Varnei said, smiling.

But he didn't step aside. Instead, he flicked both hands downwards. I saw that he had some kind of bracelet on each wrist, and in a flash, two swords were in his hands. They were curved and wicked, made from some strange white metal or bone, like fangs. Red runes traced the surface, glowing with power.

Ogen snarled again. "You really think that you can stop me? I possess power you cannot fathom, leech."

"And I've got some very pointy knives," Varnei said, shrugging, "let's see how it plays out, shall we?"

Ogen's wolf seemed to frown. Then, in an instant, the wolf vanished. It stepped forward, curling into shadow that reformed into a huge man. Ogen's human force had long white hair, a braided beard, and an eye patch over his right eye. Power thrummed from him, shadowy and strong. It spread along the beach, roiling behind him in a cloak of shadow. He wore silver-grey iron armor, like a viking. I could see runes scratched into the surface, and his power glowed through them, white like moonlight. He shifted seamlessly from wolf to man, and strode forward on the beach.

"No closer," Varnei said.

Ogen smiled and kept walking. He raised his hands. "Will you hide behind your pet leech, Anastasia? Or will you face me?"

My eyes narrowed. *I can't stop him. But maybe I can stall him enough for Ace to get here.*

I stepped out from behind Varnei.

"I'm right here, Ogen. I'm not hiding."

He grinned again. "There she is. Have you missed me, my dear?"

I shuddered. Some memory threatened to resurface, breaking against the memory wipe spell I'd been suggested to. I saw Ogen standing over me in his human form, single eye gleaming. I shook the memory away.

"There it is. Do you remember our time together? Have the memories returned?" He asked.

I grimaced; a shock of pain erupted in my right temple, followed by flashing images: Tara, casting a spell over me, staring into my eyes. I saw Ogen, prodding me with a wooden staff, and feeling pain as electricity crackled through me. *Open the gate!* He hissed.

I winced again, and when I opened my eyes, Ogen was smiling at me. "Yes… you see it now. Such fun, we had together. And of course, you've met Tara by now."

To Ogen's right, a fox appeared. It was smaller than the wolves around it, with red-brown fur and a narrow snout. The the fox to burst into flame, then reformed as the figure of a slender, red-haired woman.

Tara stepped up behind Ogen, her eyes downcast. "There you are. I do love my pet witches," he said, "so knowledgable, so passionate, so useful. You would have been an excellent addition to my collection, if you had been more cooperative."

"I'll never help you," I said. I felt my magic surging, but held it in.

Ogen smirked. "If only you knew how much you already have," he said, "you've acquired the gate opening spell from within Castle Rock. You've even drawn the sigils, creating the framework for my gate. Soon, the rest of my pack will cross into the mortal world, and I shall rule again."

I frowned. *Probably should have thought of that before we*

created the sigils, I thought.

"Doubtless, your plan is to send me back to the Fae, is that it? Clever, but ultimately foolish. That would require you having the power to defeat me in combat, and force me through the gate. And clearly, that is not the case."

He let out a low chuckle, and the sand around his feet seemed to shake with power.

I looked from him to the green glass of the gate-runes. "You need me," I said, "that's why you kidnapped me in the first place. You can't open the gate without me. You won't hurt me."

Ogen frowned. "I wouldn't be so confident, child. Hurting you might be the only way to get what I want; that's what we did the first time, anyway. Tortured you until you complied. I am willing to do that again, if you will not cooperate. Of course, torturing you made you lash out and kill many of my wolves. But the sacrifice was worth it."

I gritted my teeth. Fear flickered in my belly, threatening to crawl its way out of my throat. Was that why I was covered in blood when I woke up? He'd tortured me until I'd killed some of his pack mates? "If that is what it takes to keep you powerless, then come and get me."

To my surprise, Ogen laughed. "Ha! She's gotten even more spirited since her little stay in our camp. But you are sorely mistaken, Anastasia. There is another way to use your power, with or without your consent."

I narrowed my eyes. "What do you mean?"

"Surely by now you have heard of the Fae Queen Larien, and our brief time together. She was spirited too, you know. But in the end, I killed her and absorbed her power. And if you do not cooperate, I will do the same to you. Then no one will stand between me and my army, and the Wolf God's power will become legend!"

He raised his spear in the air at this, and his pack howled. Even Tara's eyes glowed red, his power pulsing through his pack.

Kill me and take my power. That's his plan. I felt at the spell, on the scroll in my hands. *It has to be now,* I thought.

I opened my mouth to speak, to push my power through the scroll and into the sigils on the ground. But my words died in my mouth.

A wave of force slammed into me, and I flew backwards across the beach, turning in the air. The scroll flew from my hands, crashing near the icy water of the lake. I landed, breath forced out of my lungs, my arm twisting at a painful angle.

When I looked up, Tara had stepped forward, extended her hand. Red power glowed there, wisping through her fingers.

"Oh, child. You have no idea how doomed you are," Ogen said.

And then he charged.

CHAPTER 25

Ogen raced towards me, pounding across the sand. His pack followed, howling for my blood. Ogen quickly shifted into his wolf form, a hulking beast the size of a small bus. I lifted my hand to cover my face, ready for the first bite, when I heard a snarl up ahead.

Varnei had leapt onto Ogen's back and driven his glowing bone blades into his neck. Ogen thrashed, trying to buck him off, but Varnei rode him like a prize bull, digging his blades in deeper.

But Tara and Ogen's pack still raced towards me, kicking up sand in their wake. Then Selena was in front of me, her hands aglow with green power. She raised them, and a wall of sand lifted from the beach, pressing towards the oncoming pack like a storm. Tara and the wolves were thrown back, tumbling across the sand.

"Go!" Selena yelled, "open the gate!"

I scrambled to my feet just as Selena raised spears of sand and flash fired them into glass. She thrust them at the charging wolves, striking the enemy wolves with her shards. They yelped and howled, and blood sprayed on the beach.

I ran towards the water, where the scroll lay on the shore. I dove for it, but a spray of fire illuminated the beach before me. The fireball hit, and I was thrown sideways, into the cold water. I hit the surface and the iciness of it shocked me, made my limbs twitch and shiver. I gasped, pushing my head above water and flicking my hair from my eyes. Warm air filled my lungs, and I blinked to see Tara standing on the shore, wreathed in flame. In her right hand she held the scroll.

"Whoops," she said, shaking it, "you're all wet. Let me dry you off."

She raised her hands and the surface of the lake burst into flame. The fire encircled me, keeping me trapped as I tried to stand.

"For what it's worth, it's nothing personal," she said.

"Yeah, well. I fucked your mate," I said.

She blinked, then sneered. "Okay. Now it's personal."

Her eyes flickered with power, and the flames around me burned brighter.

Then, a flash. Tara was pushed to the side, tackled by something dark and moving fast. I blinked, and the flames dimmed on a little. Then, Tara was down on the beach, a huge wolf pinning her to the sand.

Ace! I thought.

He snarled, his snout close to Tara's face.

"Hello, honey," she said.

Ace's wolf snapped at her face. "Bitch," he said, his wolf lips curling over the word.

"Harsh words so quickly. And here I thought we could still be friends," she said, pouting. "Oh, well. I see you've already moved on," she said. Then her hands and eyes glowed red, and a wall of power hit Ace, throwing him into the air. He slid to stop twenty feet down the beach, teeth bared.

Tara stood, smirking. But then she frowned, looking at her empty hands.

"Looking for something?" Ace's wolf growled. He ducked his nose down, and I saw the scroll pressed under his paw.

Then, from the woods on the shore, another howl. This one was followed by a chorus of other sounds: a bear's roar, a jaguar's scream. I looked to the woods and saw a host of shifters perched on the dunes, led by a golden mountain lion. *Grayson,* I thought.

Tara looked to them, to the town that she was sworn to protect.

"The game is up," Ace's wolf said, "they know, Tara."

Her face screwed into a snarl, "It won't matter when One Eye rules. All you did is seal their fate as traitors!" She screamed. Then she hurled a fireball at Ace. I screamed, reaching forward. The water swirled around me, and I surged out of the lake, carried on a wave. I crashed onto the shore, pulling the water around us like a cocoon. The fireball hit my shield and the water erupted into steam.

Tara looked at us. "You love too quickly, Ana," she said, "you'll realize he's not worth it in the end, just like I did. Nice dick. No ambition."

"Better than trash pussy and trash goals," I said, shrugging, "in my opinion, he dodged a bullet."

Tara's mouth dropped, and power flared in her hands. I let the water around me rise up, curling it into spears of ice.

"No!" Ace barked, "I'll take care of her. Take the scroll and open the gate!"

"But Ace!" I started. *He's no match for Tara*, I thought.

"Go!" He snarled. And he charged towards Tara. I watched him grow as he did, his wolf form swelling with power. Blue lightning crackled around him and he collided with Tara's wards, bursting through them in a shatter of broken magic.

The storm is still inside him. He'll be okay.

I dug my feet into the sand and sprinted towards the sigils. All around me, new friends clashed, risking their lives for me. Tara and Ace, Varnei and Ogen, now flanked by the shifters of Myston. Selena summoned ropes of sand and tried to bring Ogen down, but his titanic form broke free, bucking Varnei free. He slid to a stop on the beach, bloodied and cracked, his stone skin marred by Ogen's bite marks.

It has to be now, I thought. I rolled open the scroll and began to chant the words. All around me, the world crashed down. I heard screams and saw sprays of blood; Grayson's claws sank into Ogen's back, his lion form snarling.

I began to chant the words. Each one felt ancient and foreign on my tongue. *"Alieth lothlorial erelian laylia thariel ha'eseth, nimonorian vaneteria sempas!"*

The glass of the sigils glowed, this time with the cerulean light of my power. Time seemed to stop, and gravity diminished, making my hair float around me, my eyes glowing blue. I felt my feet lift off the ground, and power unlike any I'd ever known flowed through me. It was greater than the storm, greater tenfold than my own magic. It was faerie magic, god magic; as effortless as the rain and the sea and the storm. I watched as the sand and water swirled around the sigils. My voice kept reading the words of power, but my voice took on the resonance of something deeper. All around me, the battle on the beach slowed. Warriors stopped to watch the tower of light flowing upwards from the sigils. I heard screams and shouts, but couldn't hear them over the divine hum of my own power.

"Get her!" I heard Ogen cry, "stop her before the ritual is done!"

He shrew a shoulder and Grayson was thrown from him, hitting the stone of the bridge with a sickening crunch. "No!" I cried.

Wolves ran towards me, leaping at my feet, trying to pull me down, to stop my magic from opening the gate. But crackles of lightening left my body, arcing towards them, and they disintegrated in mid air. I watched as their ashes joined the swirl of power around me. Then, before me, in the tower of light, images began to show: a fairy tale landscape, all mountains and forests and glens, with a single castle rising in the distance. Bright blue skies filled with birds, and ruined walls arcing through ancient woods. *The Fae.*

"Now!" I said, "push him through!"

Selena, fatigued, barely standing, raised her arms for one last spell. Green light poured from her, and the sand under Ogen's feet began to slide towards the gate, dragging him towards the Fae.

Tara and Ace were still locked in battle, her spells glancing off of him. Then, in a single, powerful swipe, he head-butted her in the chest. She went flying towards the gate, vanishing in the blue light.

"*No!*" she screamed as she disappeared, thrown into the Fae.

Ace stopped, eyes wide with horror, panting, shifting back to him human form. He knelt, exhausted and covered in cuts and bruises, unable to stand.

No, no, no! I thought.

I opened the gate wider, and my power began to draw in Ogen's pack — blue streams of energy reached out like tentacles, grabbing wolves and sucking them into the vortex under my control. They howled and vanished, sent back to the Fae from whence they came. But for all my power, Ogen resisted me. He dug his claws into the sand, resisting both my power and Selena's spell.

Ogen shifted back into his human form, still armor clad, and thrust his spear into the ground. He knelt there, ignoring the tempest rising around him. A bear shifter swiped at him with a claw, but he drew his sword and sliced the bear in half. Both bloody halves tumbled into the Fae, sucked by the power of the portal. Other shifters threw themselves at him, and they fell in turn, killed or maimed or sent flying into the Fae.

I'm killing them, I thought, *I need to close the portal!*

Then, from nowhere, a huge half-lion form bursting from the dark. Grayson lunged at Ogen in his hybrid form, claw-like hands closing around his throat. He tackled Ogen forward, and the two of them tumbled into the portal, vanishing into the blue wall of light.

"No!" I screamed. But it was too late. Grayson and Ogen had vanished.

I tried to pull Grayson back out of the portal, but the power was too far out of my control. The gate continued to pull in everything around it, sand and sea and shifter alike. I watched as Ace, unconscious, began to slide towards the tower of light. *You're going to trap all of them in the Fae!* I thought, but the power overwhelmed me.

"I'm so sorry," I whispered.

Then, suddenly, a prick in my neck. I felt stone-strong hands around me, and could hear a cool voice whisper in my ear. Something cold and chemical spread through my neck. A sedative.

"Shh, now," Varnei said, "time to sleep."

And then, power still coursing through me, the night vanished and the blue portal dimmed into darkness.

CHAPTER 26

The world was dark for what seemed like days; I came in and out of sleep, consciousness never fully forming. Dreams replaced wakefulness replaced dreams. I dreamed of Ogen torturing me, of Tara's flames burning me, of Grayson's scream as he plunged into the Fae. I woke up in a cold sweat in the dark one night, and heard voices outside. I was still delirious, but could barely make out the voices of Ace and Selena.

"...Too much power. It nearly killed her."

"She saved the island," Ace said, his voice reverberating in my skull.

"She's too powerful. She needs to be watched," Selena said, "we both love her. But something else is going on here. We'll protect her as best we can. But until she learns to control this gift, we need to be careful. Ogen was just the beginning."

I fell back into a restless dream. I dreamed again of the ocean, of storms blasting waves, of tsunamis destroying cities. Then ice, glaciers moving over the earth, packs of wolves hunting in the endless dark. I saw a dark shape among them, sharp teeth and snow-shite skin, black hair flowing about him like a cloak. My king. My lord. My lover.

Come to me, Anastasia, he said, *come home.*

I opened my legs for him, and he slid his ice-cold cock inside of me, giving me the greatest pleasure I'd ever known. *Yes, Farien. Yes, yes!*

I woke in a start. My sheets were soaked, with arousal and sweat. I sat up, head aching.

The room was bright with daylight. I recognized it as Tara's cabin: wooden walls and ancient drapes, kitschy decorations and a stack of fresh laundry on the dresser. A plate of steaming food sat on the bedside table, eggs and sausage and coffee all mingling in the air. My nose twitched at it, and I realized I was starving. At the same time, the thought of food made me queasy. Every muscle ached and my blood felt thick, like I had the worst hangover in the world. I pushed myself up onto one arm.

"Whoah, whoah — take it easy there," a voice said. I turned to see Ace, waking up in the chair next to the bed. He moved towards me, putting a hand on my shoulder. "You should rest."

"Have you been sleeping next to my bed?" I asked.

He shrugged. "I couldn't help myself. Every time I tried to leave, my wolf took over. It's pretty attached."

"Wonder why," I said.

He smiled. "Seriously. Rest. Here, there's food and water. I can feed you…"

He reached for the fork. "I think I'll draw the line at literal spoon-feeding, thanks," I said.

He grinned sheepishly. "Right. Right," he said.

"What happened?" I asked.

"It's complicated," he said. "I can't explain all the magic. Selena basically said you lost control of the power of the Gate. Then Varnei sedated you to stop your magic from swallowing the whole island. I threw Tara through, but a few shifters got sucked in too. Ogen is gone, though. Forever."

"Grayson," I said.

He swallowed, then looked down. "Yeah," he said.

"He sacrificed himself. For us," I said.

"He was a good man. He loved us," he said.

You don't know the half of it, I thought.

"Is there any chance he's still alive?" I asked.

Ace shrugged. "He got sucked into the Fae with Ogen. Do

you think he'd let him live?"

I shuddered, knowing that Grayson had probably been slaughtered the moment the portal closed.

"Who else?" I said.

"Paul, the school teacher. Bear shifter. Alice and Ben Gleeson, both wolves. A few more. Let's not talk about that right now. The important thing is that we did it, Ana. Ogen is gone. You're safe. Myston is safe."

Am I? Or is it just the beginning?

"Varnei?" I asked.

Ace frowned. "Alive. But he took a nasty beating, for a vampire of the Stoneskin Clan. Ogen was too powerful. What did you do to make him fight for us?"

I swallowed. *I can't tell him the truth.* "Pulled in a few favors," I said, then quickly changed the subject. "If Tara is gone, who is leading Myston?"

"Right now, me. I'm the sheriff, so command goes to me if the Mayor dies. We'll have a vote soon."

"Will you run?" I asked.

"Tara always said I was too stupid to run the town," he said.

"No offense, but Tara was a bitch. And I think you proved that you were always the real leader of Myston last night," I said.

He smiled. "You're just saying that because you think I'm sexy," he said. He wiggled his eyebrows. I laughed.

"Maybe," I said. "So what comes next?"

He shrugged. "Life. We've spent too long fighting. It's time to relax," he said, "settle down."

I gulped. His eyes burned with passion, and he rested a hand on my leg.

"Ace..." I started, "I don't know if I can..."

"I'm not going to try to marry you just yet," he said, "or put a litter in you. Although my wolf is basically screaming for my to try."

Something fluttered in my belly, and I felt a wetness seep between my legs.

"I've never stayed in one place for very long," I said, "I've never felt safe..."

He frowned. "I'm not asking you to stay forever. I'm just asking you to stay for now. To give this a chance," he said.

"You didn't let me finish," I said, "I've never felt safe. Until now."

He sucked in a breath. All his muscles seemed to tense.

"You make me feel safe, Ace. You make me want to try. To try and stay here for a while," I said. I smiled weakly.

Ace slid off the bed, got onto his knees. He took my hand in his and pressed his lips to it. "I promise to protect you with my life, Anastasia Walker. So long as you will have me, I will be by your side, on my knees, worshipping you."

I smiled. "Well then, you better get started," I said. I opened my legs, slowly, watching realization dawn on his face.

"Are you sure?" He said, "you're still weak."

"You'll have to be gentle," I said, "but yes, I'm sure. Let's see what you putting a litter in me would feel like."

His eyes flashed golden, his wolf clawing towards the surface. There was a wetness blooming between my legs, and I watched as Ace caught the scent of me. A low growl hummed from his throat.

"Take me, fated mate," I said.

In a gentle motion, like he was using all his restraint, he peeled off the blanket from me. I was wearing nothing but white lace panties beneath, my tanned legs bare on the sheets. He exhaled, as if seeing me like that was the most beautiful thing in the world. He traced a strong hand up one of my legs, resting just before my panties. Then he lowered his head between my legs, and breathed deeply. His eyes flashed gold again, his wolf fighting to break through at the scent of me. He growled, the power from between my legs making his body writhe with pleasure. I watched him grind his cock helplessly against the bed.

He licked the outside of my panties, savoring the moisture there. Then his teeth clenched on the fabric. He jerked his head, and I gasped as my panties ripped off of my ass. He pulled away, my ruined underwear in his mouth. Then he took them in his fist and smelled deeply. I could see his hard cock twitch against his jeans at the scent. He unbuttoned his jeans hastily, pulling out his massive cock and letting it flop onto the bed. I gasped at the sight of it, thick and smooth, with the base hidden in a patch of fur. He gave the tip a quick stroke as he smelled my panties, and I flooded with pleasure just watching him.

He began to unbutton his shirt.

"Fuck that," I said, "I want it now."

"I want to taste you first," he growled.

"And I said I want it *now*. Shove that cock in me. I want to feel you inside of me," he said.

He grinned. "Greedy, aren't you?" he said. He climbed towards me, forcing my legs above my head. His huge hands could grab my thigh almost entirely around; I felt like a rag doll underneath him, and the fear and arousal mingled until I couldn't take it any more. His cock tickled the lips of my hole, and his thumb found my clit instantly, rubbing in intoxicating circles.

I moaned, my mouth falling open. My nipples hardened under the flannel shirt I wore, and he grabbed the fabric with a single hand and ripped. Buttons flew, and the shirt came open, exposing my bare breasts to him.

"That's what I like," he growled.

"Fuck me, Ace. Fuck me, please," I said.

He continued to tease my clit, rubbing his cock on my pussy lips, just shy of forcing it in.

"Do you want it?" He said.

"Yes, please. Fuck me already!"

"Tsk, tsk. So impatient," he said, "say pretty please."

I grabbed at his shirt, pulling myself towards him. My pussy closed over his cock, and we both cried out, the wetness and warmth overpowering us.

"Fuck!" He said. Suddenly, his hand found my throat. "Did I say you could do that, girl?"

"I'm sorry," I said, "I needed it."

"You don't get to decide," he said, "but since I'm already inside of you, you won't mind if I use your pussy as I please, is that right?"

"Yes sir," I said, through his hand around my throat, "I'm yours."

"That's what I thought," he said. He began to grind into me slowly. I cried out as he plunged in again, stretching me open.

"Fuck, Ace, you're so big," I said, "I want this cock. I want this cock for the rest of my life."

"Is that so?" He said, "you want me to cum inside you? Huh? You want me to fill you up with my pups, is that it?"

"Yes, yes sir," I said, "please, fuck me."

"I know that's what you need," he said, "I'll do it for you, Ana."

He fucked me harder, in and out, his cock plunging into me, making me squirm and moan. I listened to the wet sound of him fucking me, watched his huge tan cock dig into me. I could feel him deep in my belly, his manhood too big for my small hole.

I couldn't hold it in any more, watching him look down at me, his dark eyes intense. I knew I was the most precious thing in the world to him, that even as he used and abused me, I was in control. He would do anything for me. "Fuck me harder," I said, "I'm going to cum!"

Even before the word left me, my cunt erupted in pleasure. I felt it ripple through me, stretching from toes to fingertips, a tidal wave of pleasure and pain.

He didn't stop fucking me as I came. Instead, all I could say was "Fu-u-u-u-u-u-ck!" As he pounded the word out of me in a high pitched squeal.

"I'm going to cum," he whispered. He was overwhelmed, staring at my tits, his cock pushing into my tight hole, "oh fuck, I'm going to cum already."

"Do it," I said, "cum in me. I want it."

Both of his hands gripped my throat, and he let his most powerful strokes unleash into me. I was rocking backwards, my head slamming into the headboard, the whole room shaking with the power of his abs and thighs force fucking me.

"Fuuuuuuck!" He moaned as his cock spasmed inside of me. He twitched, burying his cock inside me, every inch. I grabbed his shirt and pulled him tighter. He collapsed onto me, breathing heavy.

"Don't take it out," I said, "I want every drop."

He breathed deeply, taking in the scent of my hair. I twitched once, completely spent, euphoria flowing through me like magic.

"I love you, Anastasia Walker," he said. It almost seemed like he couldn't help it, like in his exhaustion, the truth came out.

"I love you too," I whispered.

And I meant it.

* * *

CHAPTER 27

The days passed easily. I regained my strength, and Ace cared for me better than I'd ever been cared for. I felt myself falling for him deeper, as I watched him cook in the kitchen, or work in the yard, or as we made love. We had visitors every day it seemed, people from town scrambling to get things back on track after Tara had been exposed. As everyone expected, Ace was elected mayor. He might be gentle and funny, but he was still the Alpha, and everyone looked to him in times of trouble.

After a long day of visitors and cooking and sex, we cuddled up on the couch and turned on a movie. I wondered if I could really make a life with him; if I could stay in one place long enough to settle down, have kids, play house. I'd been on the streets for so long, living a little life with Ace seemed too good to be true. But Ace made that all seem possible.

I cuddled up into his chest, enjoying the smell of him, my fingers playing with his cotton t-shirt. The movie played, but I don't think either of us really payed attention. This was the first night that we hadn't gone straight to fucking once everyone had left the house; it felt good, normal. Like we were ordinary people, just watching a movie after the end of a long day.

When the credits rolled, Ace stretched. "I'm wiped," he said, "think I'll head to bed. Care to join me?"

I smiled, looking up at his honey-chocolate eyes. *Boy,*

would I, I thought. But instead I gave him a quick kiss and shook my head. "I told myself I was going to study Tara's spell book tonight, remember?"

He nodded. "Of course," he said, kissing my forehead.

"Besides, we've already fucked three times today," I said.

"Four," he corrected.

"Four?"

"Out by the woodpile, remember? You saw me chopping wood shirtless, couldn't resist, et cetera, et cetera," he said.

"Hm. Not must have been very memorable," I said.

"Well then, maybe I'll just have to remind you," he whispered, and he leaned in for a deep kiss. He tasted like warm rain and cinnamon and man. I melted into the kiss, my body pressed tightly against his, feeling the muscles beneath his plain white t-shirt.

He stood, stretching. "If you need me, you know where to find me," he said coyly, then ran up the stairs.

"Tease!" I called after him, and I heard him laugh.

I went to Tara's office and closed the door behind me. The room was filled with witch gear: potions and spell books and components, strange contraptions and specimens and sigils. In that room were all the things a witch needed to realize her power. All the things I never had. I wondered briefly if my mother ever had such a room.

I moved to where Tara's grimoire stood on its stand. Power thrummed from it, and I'd spent the last few days removing the wards around it, finding spells lost in the pages, hidden from prying eyes.

I would need it, where I was going.

I closed the thick book and lowered it into my backpack. Inside was food for a few days, a few changes of clothes. My usual rucksack for the road. When it was totally packed, I moved to the front door, moving silently. I'd slipped a mild sedative into Ace's drink at dinner, so I hoped he was already asleep. I listened closely for the sound of his gentle snoring, and heard it coming softly through the floorboards.

I'm so sorry, Ace, I thought. *I was telling the truth. I really do love you. I wish that this could have worked.*

It was amazing how quickly someone could feel like home. Choosing to leave him — even if it was for his own good — ripped my heart out.

When I'd wiped away the last tear, I stepped out onto the porch, got in the car, and drove away.

* * *

Varnei waited on the beach where the battle had taken place. He stood in the shadows of Castle Rock, dressed in his leather coat again, white skin against black. He approached the truck as I stepped out, feeling the sand under my boots.

"You came," he said, "I must say, I'm surprised."

"I didn't have much of a choice. We made a deal," I said.

"Not everyone keeps their promises," he purred. "But I am honored that you came for me."

"I'm not here for you. I'm here for Ace. And everyone else who would die if Farien came for me," I said.

He smiled, and his porcelain teeth glinted. "Of course. Are you ready?"

I pulled the scroll from my backpack and stepped towards where the sigils were still etched in glass on the beach. I spoke the words, and a small portal opened, just large enough for the two of us. Beyond it lay a winter fairy tale, and a distant castle made of ice.

"Come," Varnei said, "let us meet your *true* fated mate."

The End

FAE GOD: A SNEAK PEEK!

I knew I was being followed as soon as I entered the tavern. I pulled my cloak closer around my head, hiding my dark hair within. Their aura was distinct: shifters. Wolves, if I had to guess. One of them might be a bear. All of them were lower ranking wolves: betas, or maybe one of the other castes. No alphas at least. What that meant, I didn't know.

I had a concealment charm etched into the fabric of my cloak — I hoped that would help. Maybe in the human world, magic would have given me away to them. But here, in the Fae, magic was everywhere. A witch on the run fit in just fine.

I'd been on the run for months. Stuck in the Fae, in the Winter King's kingdom, for two whole ass stupid months. Ever since I agreed to go with Varnei, the vampire bounty hunter, so he could collect his prize from King Farien for delivering his supposed fated mate. Well, that plan had gone to shit. Varnei was dead or gone, to where I didn't know. King Farien's men — elves, shifters, ogres — were hunting me. And to make it worse, the scroll that I used to pass between the mortal world and the Fae was gone. Burnt to a god-damn crisp.

The tavern was a dinky little thing in a village called Turnip. Stupid fucking name for town, but that's the Fae. The patrons were many, even at the early hour of… almost sundown. I had brought an electronic watch and a cellphone into the Fae, but modern technology didn't work. Too much magic around. As a result, the bar was made entirely of old wood, and dug into the side of a hill outside of Turnip. Goats grazed on the roof, although there wasn't much green to be seen in the Winter

Kingdom. Inside, candles and oil lamps lit the dim room, and a goblin stood behind the long bar, cleaning a glass.

Goblins. Elves. Ogres. Just a few months ago, I didn't believe the Fae existed. Sure, shifters were real, and so were witches (exhibit A: me) but the Fae was a fairy tale. It was right there in the name: Fae-ry Tale. But now, I was living it. And it wasn't very fun at all.

I sat in a far corner booth, back to the wall, half concealed in shadow, so that I could get a good look at the men following me. I blended in all right: I'd ditched my human clothes for something more fitting, and the cloak covered my face and hair. I wore leather pants and vest, with a wool undershirt and leather riding boots. All of it was covered in a green wool cloak, which was trimmed with wolf fur for the biting winds of the Winter Kingdom. That, and a small warming spell I'd drawn on the inside flap. My magic wasn't exactly... working. Not in the way it had in the mortal world. But small spells were still okay if I took the time to draw out the runes. Luckily, I'd thought to bring the spell book Tara had given me (before she betrayed me and tried to kill me by sacrificing me to a crazed shifter god). Oh, and before I stole her boyfriend.

Ace.

The thought of Ace made my heart stop and my stomach clench. I'd left him to hand myself over to Farien, in the hopes that he wouldn't come to Earth to find me and wind up bringing an endless winter with him. Of course, that hadn't gone to plan either.

I'd abandoned my mate.

I'd broken his heart.

And now, I was being punished for it.

Three dark shapes entered the bar. Almost instantly, the chatter stopped, and every head turned to watch them. They were three hulking shifters, wearing the cloaks of their kind: two wolves and a bear. The pelts draped over chainmail and leather, making them look like Vikings. Tattoos curved up their arms, faerunes I didn't recognize. The bear was a huge redhead, seemingly twice as tall as the two wolves. The wolves were a man and a woman, both dark haired and angular. They had scimitars and daggers at their waists, while the bear had a battle axe strapped to his back.

The wolf male scanned the bar with shimmering dark eyes. Something about his aura told me he was a high ranking beta. I didn't know who his alpha was, but I'd bet that it was Ogen One Eye.

Ogen — that was another problem. My genius plan to save the village of Myston was to send Ogen back to the Fae, where he came from. Of course I found myself trapped in the fae within a few days, with a Fae God who wants me for a bride and a Wolf God who wants me dead.

Life was going swimmingly.

The three shifters stepped forward, and I saw the lead beta's nose twitch. He was trying to scent me.

Quickly, I pulled on my magic. A more powerful concealment charm might keep me hidden long enough to escape. The blue light inside me welled, grew…

And then flickered out.

Fuck.

That was one more thing: my magic hadn't been working, in the traditional sense. I had a few spells etched into my cloak, and I could still cast using faerunes, but my magic — usually powerful water magic — didn't want to work in the Fae. I was basically helpless.

The lead shifter sniffed again, but if he scented me, he didn't give it away. Instead, he walked up to the goblin barkeep and threw a coin down on the table. "Three meads," he said. His voice was surprisingly lyrical, like a silver flute.

While he ordered the bear and the female wolf scanned the bar nonchalantly.

Her eyes floated over the goblins, elves, pixies, and then settled on me. She smiled, and I could see sharp canines. Gauche, to wear your wolf teeth around, but fashion in the Fae was less Tiffany and more Lord of the Rings.

I eyed the exits. Or, exit. There was the one door that I came through, and then there was a door to the kitchens. Given that the tavern was built into a hillside, I doubted that door lead anywhere outside.

Fuck. I was trapped.

I eyed the door again. It was about twenty feet away, and a crowd of drunk fairy tale creatures stood between me and it. I let my hand slide to the knife at my waist. *I can't take three shifters*, I thought, *not without magic.*

But maybe I can trick them.

I waited for the female shifter's eyes to move away — just for a moment as she tapped their leader on his shoulder — and then bolted.

I slipped away from the table, keeping to the shadows. My cloak still had the basic concealment charm stitched in, thanks to a lot of hard work with Tara's spell book, but it didn't make me invisible, just harder to spot. I watched the female shifter turn back to the now-empty booth, and her eyes narrowed.

"Well?" Asked the boss.

"I… er… she was…." The female muttered.

"There!" said the bear. I sighed. Now it was really starting to sound like a fairy tale.

He pointed at me with one thick, muscled and tattooed arm.

I swallowed. But I'd been in similar situations before, when I was living on the street. Given, they were human streets, but still.

I leaned over to a drunk humans sitting at the table in front of me.

They stopped laughing and cursing just long enough to listen. "Did you guys hear? Those three shifters at the bar just called you a bunch of furless, wimpy, good for nothing lushes! Can you believe that?"

The drunkest of the men in front of me blinked twice, then scowled. "They said what?"

"They said you were peltless, disgusting, humans. I might be a bleeding heart, but I just can't tolerate that kind of talk."

If only I could use a glamour. It would make this whole process easier. Still, the drunkest of them stood, grabbed his half sword from his waist, and began to stumble over to my pursuers.

"Oh, no!" I said, putting on my best damsel-in-distress act. "He's going to get himself killed. Someone do something!"

The rest of his companions — a motley crew of fairly drunk mercenaries, stood up and charged the three shifters. Their table flipped over, spilling mead and beer all over the tavern floor, and the other patrons. By then, half the bar was up in arms, looking for someone to fight.

Perfect.

I ran towards the door, through the chaos, and threw myself through it just as I heard the roar of a bear shifter that was seriously pissed off.

The chaos of the tavern brawl vanished, and was replaced with the bustling Main Street of Turnip. The whole village was built into a series of hills, and the Main Street — more like an alley, really, because they didn't have cars here — twisted between them. Little houses and house-holes were bored into the hills, all covered in snow. People and creatures of all types went about their business: catfolk farmers sold winter vegetables, orc blacksmiths pounded metal by their forges, and pixie merchants sold baubles of jewelry.

I took off through the crowded Main Street, hoping that the myriad scents might confuse my pursuers. I weaved and bobbed, and once I was out of sight, I slipped off my cloak and tucked it into my satchel. At the very least, a wardrobe change might distract them. I wanted to pull my dad's leather jacket out and wear it, at least for the comfort, but something so distinctly mortal couldn't help me blend in. Instead, I tucked my long black hair under a cap, hoping to pass as a man — not that my ass would ever let that happen.

I ducked into an alleyway and made the change.

That's when I heard his voice.

"Anastasia Walker," the beta shifter said. He appeared out of the shadows of the alleyway, all lithe muscles and smooth black leather. His wolf pelt's dead eyes stared at me hungrily.

I backed up, ready to make a run for it, when I slammed into something rock solid. Muscled arms wrapped around me, and I looked up into the face of the thuggish bear shifter, his grin showing pearly white teeth.

"Let go of me!" I shouted. I reached for my magic again, but the blue light flickered away when I tried to touch it. Instead, I reached for my dagger — only for a thin feminine hand to grab my wrist. I turned to see the female wolf — sharp, beautiful features and flowing dark hair — smiling at me. She took my dagger, inspected it, and, unimpressed, threw it at the wall next to me. It stuck in the wood, reverberating. "Cute," she purred.

The bear shifted turned me around, his arms locking mine in place. I spat stray hair out of my face and looked at the beta stalking towards me. He touched my face, turning me to face him.

"So... ordinary," he said. His voice was delicate for a shifter, sophisticated. I don't know why everyone in the Fae has a kind-of-but-not-really British accent."Surprising, that she should be desired so. But still. Lord Farien wants what he wants."

He smiled, and I saw a gold tooth glitter in the lamplight.

"Well. Best not to keep your groom to be waiting," he said. Then he reached into his pocket, pulled out a handful of green dust, and threw it in my face. Before I could even question what it was, the world around me sunk into a pitch black sleep.

ABOUT THE AUTHOR

Lily Tate

Lily Tate lives in Minnesota with her rescue mutt and (non magic) boyfriend. She spends her time creating worlds filled with hot alpha shifters, dark fae kings, and badass magical heroines.

BOOKS BY THIS AUTHOR

Wolf God

Fae God